"Grace, I'm not who you think I am."

"What? What are you talking about?"

"I mean, I'm not really one of the good guys. I'll keep you and Mikey safe from Serrano, but you need to keep yourself safe from me."

"You're not making any sense, Sam."

"Listen to me. A long time ago I let my family down. Slithered off when they needed me most. If you get too close, I'll only let you down, too. Let me keep to myself and do my job."

"I don't buy any of that for one moment. If you're not one of the good guys, I don't know who is. And as far as letting you 'keep to yourself,' if you're talking about our kiss, both of us wanted that kiss and you know it. So no good 'keeping to yourself,' pal. You brought us here, now live with the consequences."

Dear Reader,

I have a wonderful new series for you! *Texas Baby Sanctuary* is the first book in my Chance, Texas miniseries, my opportunity to travel back to my old home in Texas, at least for a while. Chance is the name of a small west Texas town, and it's also the name of the large ranching family that owns most of the county. I couldn't wait to write another Texas series. About a family filled with rugged cowboys who live in small-town Texas. What's not to love?

Texas Baby Sanctuary is U.S. marshal Sam Chance's story. He's the oldest son and has been gone from home a long time. In this book he returns in order to save a woman and her child from a fierce drug lord. Grace Baker is trying to save her baby from the clutches of his dangerous father. Grace doesn't know whom to trust, and finally turns to Sam for help. Meanwhile Sam has troubles of his own. When he left home he burned a lot of bridges, and now he must come back to ask for help.

I hope you enjoy *Texas Baby Sanctuary* as Grace and Sam strive for their own chance at happiness.

Happy reading,

Linda

LINDA CONRAD

Texas Baby Sanctuary

ROMANTIC

SUSPENSE

Recycling programs
for this product may
not exist in your area.

ISBN-13: 978-0-373-27772-8

TEXAS BABY SANCTUARY

Printed in U.S.A.

LINDA CONRAD

When asked about her favorite things, Linda Conrad lists a longtime love affair with her husband, her sweetheart of a dog named KiKi and a sunny afternoon with nothing to do but read a good book. Inspired by generations of storytellers in her family and pleased to have many happy readers' comments, Linda continues creating her own sensuous and suspenseful stories about compelling characters finding love.

A bestselling author of more than twenty-five books, Linda has received numerous industry awards, among them the National Reader's Choice Award, the Maggie, the Write Touch Readers' Award and the RT Book Reviews Reviewers' Choice Award. To contact Linda, to read more about her books or to sign up for her newsletter and/or contests, go to her website, www.lindaconrad.com.

To everyone who has ever dreamed of finding happiness with a cowboy.

Chapter 1

Stinging cold rain ran off the brim of his hat and dripped down the back of U.S. Marshal Sam Chance's neck.

Shrugging deeper into his lambskin coat, Sam felt chilled through and bone weary. So flipping bone weary, in fact, that he figured sleeping for a hundred years would make a great way to spend his next time off—whenever that might happen.

But as he stood on the pavement in the rough March drizzle staring through the smudged front window of a run-down highway café, his body got a shot of much-needed adrenaline. And suddenly he had no need for sleep anytime soon.

She was there. Bending over to wipe down an empty table. After searching for the past six weeks, he'd finally found his woman.

The information he'd obtained from those truck drivers a few days ago had been the key to finding her. They'd said she was working as a waitress in this dingy joint. And there she was.

But look at how fragile she seemed from this distance. He'd never known her to be so thin. And she'd changed her hair color again. He had grown rather partial to the bright red, but he supposed honey-blond was not all bad—if what you needed the most from your hair color was a temporary disguise.

Where was her baby? Did she bring him to work with her? Was the child in the back room of the café?

Wanting to go to her, to hear her voice again, he fisted his hands at his sides instead and tried to clear his mind.

But he didn't move. He didn't as much as blink an eyelash. Focusing his eyes past the leftover Christmas decorations on the window, that were by now looking pretty ratty, he simply gazed at her.

He shouldn't be here. Never should have started this quest to find her in the first place. He'd taken a leave from his job in order to begin the search. But now that he'd found her, he couldn't take his eyes off her. That she was still well and breathing free air felt like such a relief he could barely think.

It had been days since he'd gotten any sleep. What would he have done if something had happened to her? If she'd died or disappeared for good? It would have killed him, too, knowing it had been his duty to protect her and her child from harm, but that he'd let them slip away.

Yeah, his boss had been right when he'd said it was her own problem. Once witnesses leave the Security Program, the safety of their very lives lands back in their own hands. But those rules didn't seem to matter to Sam. His boss even went so far as to suggest that he had taken too much of a personal interest.

Nonsense. He just felt a responsibility for her. Though she was a beautiful woman, and he wasn't dead—

But dang, it had been fairly easy for him to find her. That meant the bad guys wouldn't have much problem locating her, either. She was in mortal danger, that's all there was to it.

Just as that thought crossed his mind, the hairs on the back of his neck stood straight up. Something felt wrong. He absently touched the weapon in the holster inside his jacket and turned to look around. Except for a couple of old pickups the parking lot seemed empty in the early evening drizzle. The West Texas wind howled down the highway out in front like a train's horn blaring through a tunnel.

Not a fit night for man or beast. His father's words from long ago rang in his memory.

He figured it must be the familiar, yet unhappy, atmosphere of this West Texas town and the surrounding area that was making him feel so jittery all of a sudden. Or maybe it was the guilt of knowing he shouldn't have come on this rescue at all. Being here could easily cost him his job.

Turning back to the café, he forced himself to move toward the front door. With one more quick glance over his shoulder he assured himself he was alone and pushed at the door handle.

It was time to make Ms. Grace Baker see the light. She couldn't manage this all on her own. And he was just the right man to convince her of that fact.

Grace hauled her last load of dishes into the kitchen, trying her best to put one foot in front of the other. The feet that were killing her. Ten more minutes until closing time. Charlie the cook, also her boss, had left five minutes ago and she was supposed to lock up. She could make it.

She'd never done much manual labor, not until the past six months when her whole life had been tossed in the air like a salad. But this was good, *honest* work. And it almost provided a living for her and her baby. Grace was proud of what she'd accomplished so far.

And she didn't mind living here in Fort Stockton. The kind couple who ran the café had given her a job and a temporary place to live, hadn't they? Even the customers weren't too bad. The long-haul drivers left great tips and the locals spoke to her as if they'd known her all their lives.

Knowing she couldn't linger in this town indefinitely, there were still times when Grace wished she could stay. Stay somewhere. Anywhere where she and the baby would be safe.

She'd better stop wishing for the impossible and finish off her shift. Pushing back through the swinging kitchen door into the dining room, she noticed the café had a new customer and he was standing with his back to the door. As she opened her mouth to tell him the café was almost closed, he lifted his chin and their eyes met. Her breath caught in her throat.

Only one pair of sky-blue eyes in the whole world could affect her that way. Brooding and unreadable, those eyes stared at her from beneath the brim of a soaked white Stetson. They belonged to a man she recognized all too well.

Sam Chance. Marshal Sam Chance. She froze in place, not knowing whether to feel relief or to turn and run. He'd found her—after all her efforts to stay lost.

"Evening, Grace. We need to talk." Sam's voice still carried that slow, deep, sensual tone that had hypnotized her from the beginning.

Her mouth went dry. Her skin tingled. She was torn with indecision.

Sam represented security and a chance for a real life. But it was also possible that he posed a huge threat to her well-being and to the safety of her son. Much as she didn't want to think it, Sam may have been the leak, the one that had brought danger ever closer to her and Mikey six weeks ago.

Just at that moment the door at Sam's back opened and her worst nightmare stepped inside. Two dark men holding big menacing-looking guns. And they were definitely coming in her direction.

Sam had led the wolves right to her door!

Sam watched carefully as Grace noticed him. At first that wary look in her eyes seemed to soften when she realized who he was. But then her eyes widened, darkened. And sudden fear pulled at the corners of her lips, turning her mouth down into a grimace.

By the time he'd felt the air shift as the door opened behind him, Sam was already reaching for his weapon. He gave the café a quick visual check and found it empty save for him and Grace—and whatever danger lurked at his back.

The situation called for a couple of fast and lethal maneuvers if they were going to walk away from this, and he didn't want any innocent bystanders getting hurt. Grace couldn't be hurt, either. But that would take a bit more finesse.

Springing toward her, he body blocked her out of the line of fire. "Run! Out the back."

The first bullet zipped past his ear as he skidded across the tile floor and crashed headfirst into chairs then a table. He righted himself and reached for cover. Overturning the table to use as a shield, he dropped to one knee just as he caught sight of Grace ducking through the door to what must be the kitchen.

Sam knew the kitchen had a back way out because he'd parked his SUV in the alley and had seen the door. He didn't want her going outside without his protection. But for now he needed to stop the threat right here before he caught up to her.

Another thump hit the wall behind his head with no discernable roar of a discharged weapon, telling Sam that the bullet had come from a silenced handgun. He aimed his own forty-five and blasted off a couple of shots. The noise of gunfire reverberated through the café, and the flash from his muzzle as he fired his first shot gave away his position.

He needed a lucky break. And then he got one.

One of the shooters stepped away from his cover to take better aim. Sam stared down the barrel at him and fired, catching the man in the chest. The fellow yelped and slumped to his knees.

The injured man's partner turned to see how badly his buddy had been hit, and Sam used the lull from the other side of the room to fire the rest of the bullets in his magazine. Ducking, the uninjured partner crawled to his comrade instead of returning fire. As Sam reloaded, he spotted the one assailant hugging the walls while he struggled to drag his partner toward the front door.

Good enough. Sam used the opportunity to sprint in the opposite direction toward the kitchen. Protecting Grace was his first priority.

Barging through the swinging door, he looked

around, expecting to find Grace and her baby huddled in a corner. But the tiny kitchen was empty. *Damn it, Grace. You can't do this on your own.*

He vaulted over a couple of counters and scrambled to the door under the exit sign. Flattening himself to the wall just inside, he used the threshold as cover while he turned the knob and pushed open the door. He glanced out at an angle and saw Grace tugging frantically at the door handle of his SUV. It was the only thing within view that she could use as a cover, but he'd locked it before coming inside.

Only a matter of fifty feet lay between them, but Sam wasn't sure his heart could take the beating before he reached her. As he ran he heard another engine starting up nearby. He hoped to hell their assailants were heading off to find a hospital, but he wasn't ready to stake his life on that possibility.

He hit the SUV's remote door-unlock button while making a dash for it. By the time he reached the vehicle, Grace already had one leg inside. He launched himself at the open door and carried her with him as he dove into the driver's seat.

They landed in a jumble of arms and legs and it took him a second to straighten out and shove her into the passenger seat. "Where's the baby?"

Grace worked to fasten her seat belt, but she narrowed her lips and remained silent.

"Where is Mikey, Grace?"

"My son is safe. *You* stay away from him." She folded her arms over her chest and stared out the window.

The bitterness and fear in her voice ripped at his gut. But he didn't have time to argue with her. She had good reason not to trust too easily. He would ask again when he was sure he could keep both of them alive.

He cranked the key and the SUV's engine roared to life. "Hang on, they haven't given up yet."

In his side mirror he caught sight of a four-door pickup with oversize tires as it swung around in the street out front and headed their way. Ramming the SUV in gear, he locked his jaw, hit the gas and took off.

Two seconds later he downshifted around a corner in a screeching, careening, two-wheeled turn. Punching the accelerator once again and shifting straight into fourth gear, he sent them flying down a short city block.

"Are you trying to kill us?" Grace gasped as she clutched at the inside door handle.

"I can lose 'em. Just keep holding tight."

Buildings flew by in a fuzzy blur, but Sam made the SUV scream while he raced down the straightaway. The next four corners were exercises in steel nerves as he ran stoplights, dodged cars and took another ninety-degree turn into a narrow alley.

Breathing hard, he sandwiched the SUV into a small slot behind two garbage Dumpsters and idled the engine. With his eyes glued on both the rearview mirror and the street out the windshield, he gave it a tense five minutes before he took a deep breath and said anything.

"That pickup had Mexican plates. You know what it means, don't you, Grace?"

Her only acknowledgment for a full moment was a slight nod of her head. "He found me. Or…" Shifting in her seat, she glared straight at him. "You led him to me."

A tiny niggle of guilt ran down Sam's spine. It was possible he'd been followed. But he was so sure he'd covered his trail.

"No. Think about it for a moment. If I could find you so could someone with as much power as Jose Serrano. You're not trained in putting the details together for a total disappearance. You're no match for the biggest drug lord along the Mexican-American border."

She turned her head away and a shaft of light from the nearby streetlamp caught her in its glow. "Don't tell me about matching wits with that bastard. I'm the one who managed to escape him and then testified at his trial and conviction. It's you and your people who can't seem to keep one step ahead of him."

Taking another cleansing breath, Sam ignored the silky sheen of her hair and the haunting smell of strawberries he had always loved about her, and tried another tactic. "Come on, Grace. You're a single mother with a child. You can't do this alone. Let me help you. Two people can better protect Mikey. I won't let Serrano get to him, I swear it."

She swung around again and narrowed her eyes. "I'm not going back to L.A. or anywhere else the government wants to put me. Not until Jose is safely returned to his prison cell. Someone in your agency must be helping him."

Sam opened his mouth to argue that the U.S. Marshals Service did not help gang informants or turncoats. But then thought better of it. It was possible she could be right. Serrano's escape from jail during trial had looked all too easy. And then it had seemed impossible that anybody could've been sniffing around trying to get information on Grace and Mikey in Denver. No one should've had access to their whereabouts in hiding except for other agents in his department. But Serrano's men had shown up in Denver just the same.

"Okay. We won't go back." His mind raced with different scenarios for keeping his two charges safe. "I won't even contact anyone in the Marshals Service to let them know where we are. I'm on leave anyway, and I have another idea."

"You're on leave? You took a leave of absence to come looking for me and Mikey? Why?"

Her voice had returned to its whiskey-smooth tone, the sound music to his ears. He loved the way she talked when she was relaxed and easygoing. Her voice rolled over him like a warm ocean wave. Maybe he could make things work out okay after all.

"I promised you when we left L.A. and put you and the baby in protective custody that I wouldn't let anything happen to you two. I don't make promises lightly, Grace. And I intend to see you have a new life that doesn't include any overhanging threats from a drug lord."

She stayed quiet for a few moments, and he could see her facial expressions as they reflected the struggle for answers that would keep her safe. He held his breath and hoped to hell she came up with the right answer soon.

"All right," she whispered at last. "I appreciate the help. But if you're lying, I swear…"

She sighed, resigned to having little choice. "Let's go get Mikey. And hurry, please. If Jose Serrano found me, he can just as easily find his own son."

Chapter 2

Grace shivered and turned up the heater as Sam started the SUV and drove at a crawl out of the alley onto a downtown street. But the deserted street that had seemed so small-town friendly in the daylight suddenly felt cold and dangerous. For the first time since she'd come here, she wished this West Texas town didn't roll up its sidewalks at nine at night in the winter.

"You're cold."

"I didn't have a chance to get my coat when I left."

Sam grimaced. "You want mine?"

"No. No, thanks. I'm feeling warmer already." She didn't want his coat in case she had to take off in a hurry. She wasn't a thief.

"We make too good a target alone in the open like this." Sam drove through the misty rain to the corner stop sign, lightly hit the brakes and turned to her. "We need to get out of town. Fast. Which way to pick up your son?"

"Left toward the main highway." As he turned the wheels, she opened her mouth to explain that Mikey was staying with a neighbor. "He's probably asleep but…"

The screech of tires behind them kept the rest of her sentence firmly stuck in her throat. Along with her heart.

"Ohmygod, they found us again!" The words exploded from her mouth.

Sam stepped on the gas and shot down the quiet street. Without a word, he made four quick right-hand turns.

"What are you doing? We're back to where we started."

He took one more right. "We're becoming the hunters instead of the prey. These guys need a nasty little surprise. And we're going to give it to them."

Grace held her breath and hung on as Sam tore up behind the black truck. He rolled down his window and pulled a gun from his coat pocket.

"Scrunch lower in your seat. Keep your head down."

She did as he said. And closed her eyes for good measure. But nothing could keep the loud cracks of gunfire from assailing her eardrums. Jerking with every round, with every ping of bullet hitting metal, she braced her feet to keep from rolling into Sam's way as the SUV swerved, braked and raced.

Between firing and driving, Sam muttered a string of four-letter curses. After their SUV took what felt to her like a one-eighty, she held on to her seat as Sam sped off with another burst of gas. They were going back the way they'd come? Running away? Fine by her.

Opening her eyes, she was surprised to see the pickup

heading straight at them. Sam fired a couple more shots out his window just as the truck passed. Then it turned off in an erratic move. Apparently her U.S. Marshal had won his game of chicken.

"I think I hit the driver on that last pass. That should keep them busy long enough for us to pick up Mikey and get out of town."

Speechless and out of breath, Grace tried to piece her scrambled brain back together. What if Mikey had been in the SUV with them during that little scene?

Not a chance. "I've changed my mind. My baby and I will leave town on our own. Thanks for the offer, but no thanks. Drop me off at my apartment."

"You…can't go back to your place now." Sam drew a ragged breath and the sound caused her to look in his direction. "What makes you think they won't be there waiting for you?"

"Why would they know where I live? But to be safe, drop me off somewhere and I'll walk back to my place. I think those characters are following you, not me."

Groaning, he muttered, "Gracie, please…"

That's when she saw it. Blood. Soaking through his coat and dripping down the limp left hand resting on the steering wheel.

"You've been shot! Stop. I'll drive you to the hospital."

He did come to a stop and turned to her. "It's really nothing. Besides, we can't show up at any hospital. That's the first place they might look. I'll find an all-night convenience store and pick up a few supplies so I can take care of it myself."

Grace wasn't crazy about staying in the SUV while they drove down public streets. And she sure as the devil was not happy about being tied to Sam this way. Serrano's men knew Sam's SUV. Maybe that's how they'd followed them in the first place.

Scared beyond reason, she came up with a plan. Sam didn't know where she lived. When he stopped at the store, she would sneak away while he was inside. She'd walk back to the apartment. Get her car and her baby and leave town before he could locate her and catch up.

She had been doing okay without him for the past six weeks. She could do okay without him in the future.

Pulling up in front of the store, he parked in the middle of a row of pickups and SUVs. "Looks like half the town wants something from the store tonight. It should give us a little cover while I get what I need."

He put the SUV in Park, but left it running. "It'll only take a minute or two. Stay warm."

Reaching for the door handle, he winced and groaned, grabbing his left shoulder. "Hell."

"You're hurt badly, Sam. Tell me what you need. I'll go." Had she really said that? There went her great plan.

But she couldn't stand to see him hurting like this and not offer to help.

He released a deep breath and stared at her. "You sure?"

"I'm sure."

After listening to his list, she turned to climb out but turned back. "Move over while I'm gone. I'll be driving from here on. We need to tend that wound of yours as quickly as possible."

"No hospitals."

She shook her head with exasperation. "Fine. No hospitals. We'll think of something else."

"Are you sure you don't want my coat?"

"I'm okay." A bloody leather coat would catch a lot

of attention she didn't want. And since she'd decided not to run, she really didn't need a coat.

Making a dash for the convenience store door, Grace chided herself for being a fool. An idiot.

Sticking with Sam could easily mean her death. But leaving him hurting like that had suddenly become the most impossible thing she'd ever attempted.

And she had to wonder why.

Sam's mind raced with wildly varying thoughts. He needed to find a way to lose those gunmen for good. More importantly he had to convince Grace to stay and let him help her.

But face it, if he were her, he wouldn't stick around, either. She'd been safe for weeks without his protection and the moment he'd showed up she was in trouble again.

Some protector he made. The idea of not being able to protect Grace sent a shiver down his back. For years he'd tried to put his past mistakes, the guilt and pain, far behind him. And he had been so all-fired-sure he had. Up until now.

This situation somehow seemed too vaguely familiar. Too much like his past. It brought up painful memories he'd worked hard to erase.

Needing to push them aside the same way he'd been doing for years and start acting in a professional manner, he forced his training and years of experience to the front of his mind. He must be smarter than the bad guys.

Why couldn't he shake the drug lord's men?

Sam was absolutely positive that no one had followed him. He was too good to let that happen. So how had they found him?

And they had found him—not Grace. That was abundantly clear.

But how?

Had to be some kind of tracking chip—the only sensible answer he could come up with. The Mexican drug lord must've stepped right into the twenty-first century and used satellite technology to locate him.

Okay. Where was the chip?

A couple of possible answers sprung to mind. His cell phone and the SUV. A tracking chip could've been secretly placed on either one with some ease.

But he didn't figure he'd be able to find something as tiny as a chip in the darkness and rain, or in a big hurry. So it looked as if he would have to do things differently. Make new plans. Starting immediately.

Grace was fuming as she left the store. It had seemed every person in the whole town had been there buying cold medicine in the middle of the night. The lines at the register had been slow and long. She had hated leaving Sam alone for such a protracted amount of time.

Looking up, she was stunned to find the SUV was not in the same parking place where it had been when she'd left. What had happened to Sam?

A moment of panic gave way to surprise. She spotted him standing in the parking lot in the drizzle next to an old, dusty pickup truck and looking as though he was waiting for her.

"What's going on? Where's the SUV?"

"I traded it for this pickup. I sure hope you can drive a stick shift, 'cause I'm not sure I'm in any shape."

"You traded a nearly new, loaded SUV for this old heap? Are you crazy?"

"No. I'm finally getting smart. Climb in the driver's

seat. We need to move." He eased himself into the passenger seat.

She could see the pain etched in the lines around his eyes. He must be really hurting to ask her to drive. This was life and death. Their lives. So she quit thinking and just moved.

The pickup's door creaked and groaned as she opened it. Piece of junk truck. Throwing her plastic bags full of drug supplies on the little half seat in back, she jumped up into the driver's seat.

Then cranking the motor, she carefully steered the truck out of the lot. "Where to? Can we go get Mikey now?"

"First I need…help…with this bleeding. The bullet was a through and through and didn't do much damage, but the bleeding won't stop." He groaned, closed his eyes and laid his head back on the headrest.

"And you still think we can't go to my place? You really believe they could find it without following us there?"

He didn't answer, just moaned and gripped his upper arm with white-knuckled fingers.

Yeah, she knew what he thought. She also knew that he needed help in a hurry.

Swinging the pickup around, she headed across the highway into a not-so-nice part of town. In two minutes they were driving past auto mechanics' garages, ancient diners and sleazy motels. She picked a motel that at least looked well tended from the outside.

"Hang on a sec." She put on the parking brake and left the truck running while she ran inside the motel office to register.

But within minutes she was back and opening the

truck's passenger door. "Sam, do you have any cash? They insist on money up front."

He winced and tried to move, but finding it too painful, he said, "Inside jacket pocket. Take what you need."

Carefully she slid her hand inside his coat and reached into his pocket. But when she pulled out a fistful of bills and found them to be fifties and hundreds, she gulped down her surprise. What was he doing carrying so much cash?

Taking only what was needed, she replaced the rest and ran back to get the key.

The real trick was getting Sam out of the truck and into the motel room. He stood at least a half foot taller and had maybe sixty or seventy pounds on her. But Sam helped as much as he could and eventually they were locked inside, with him sprawled out on the bed and her fighting to remove his jacket.

By the time the jacket was hanging over the back of the lone chair in the room, Grace was sweating and huffing.

Then she looked at the wound on his arm and felt sick to her stomach. Nasty-looking tear, but by now it only oozed a trickle of blood.

"I have to clean the wound and use the antibacterial cream before we can bandage. It's going to hurt, Sam. Is that okay?"

He opened his eyelids and stared up at her. "Do what's necessary. I trust you."

Their gazes met, held. Through his clearly visible pain, she saw something else. An emotion she hadn't ever seen in Sam's eyes before. An emotion she wasn't sure she'd ever seen in anyone's eyes when they looked at her.

It was something she wasn't sure she deserved: *re-*

spect. And the sight so unnerved her that she broke the awkward moment and turned away.

She did what she could for the wound. But not being a trained nurse, she had to pray the bandage would hold back any further bleeding and yet not be so tight that it cut off the circulation to his hand. Next she gave him a couple of Tylenol, hoping that would help with his pain.

When it was all over, she said, "You need rest. Sleep. At least a couple of hours. Can I use your cell phone to call Mikey's sitter? She can keep him overnight, but I need to let her know."

"I tossed it into the truckbed of a Ford F-150 with Oklahoma plates. It's probably a hundred miles from here by now. No phone in this room?" His eyes were still closed and she wasn't sure he could focus if he opened them.

"You threw your phone away? Why?"

Opening his eyes, he reached out and grabbed her hand. "Determined to lose those bastards. I would do anything to save you and Mikey. Whatever it takes."

He held her hand so tightly, it almost hurt. And he was giving her another strange look. A look that said she mattered.

Flustered and not at all sure what she felt, Grace tried to back out of his grip. "Sleep, Sam. Don't worry about a thing. It'll all look different in the morning."

Dropping her hand and closing his eyes, Sam immediately fell into a deep sleep. Grace looked down on him, and absently worked a palm across the ache that had developed in the vicinity of her chest.

No one but Mikey had ever trusted her so completely as to fall asleep in her presence. She was amazed by the confusing kinds of feelings that kind of trust brought up inside her.

She tugged off Sam's boots and slipped a clean-looking blanket over his still-dressed form. For now she needed to put emotions aside and do what was needed. First find a phone, then watch over Sam as he slept to be sure his wound didn't become infected and cause a fever.

She couldn't let him down. His trust in her would not be misplaced. At least not for tonight.

Chapter 3

A loud bang jerked Sam out of a deep sleep. Sitting straight up in bed, he tried to get his bearings.

Was that a gunshot? He reached for his weapon before realizing he wasn't wearing his jacket.

No coat. He must be in bed. Whose bed? Blinking the fuzziness out of his eyes and shaking his head, Sam started to swing his feet over the side.

The ache in his left shoulder pulled him up short. Oh, yeah. He'd been shot—just winged, really. But the loss of blood had left him weak.

He heard a key going into the door lock. Someone was coming. Forcing his feet to the ground, he stood and looked around for something to use as a weapon.

"You're up. How are you feeling?" Grace, arms loaded with plastic bags, kicked the door closed behind her.

She looked up at him with a sunny expression and those big, wide eyes he had always been a sucker for.

"Nothing wrong with me." He checked his watch while waiting for his heartbeat to settle. Ten in the morning. Hell.

"I brought you some orange juice and heavy-duty painkillers." She handed him the orange juice carton and a couple of pills. "The pharmacist says you need to stay hydrated and rest for a couple of days until you get your strength back."

"Screw resting. And screw these pills. I've been out cold for twelve hours. Enough. We need to leave town. Where's Mikey?"

"He's fine. Still with the neighbor. I ran by and saw him this morning. Told them I'd be back to pick him up in a couple of hours."

Sam drank half the orange juice straight from the carton. "No sign of Serrano's men?"

Grace shook her head. "I also went by my apartment—before daybreak. But I parked around the corner and walked there the back way. I changed clothes and cleaned out as much as I could carry before telling my boss and his wife that I was quitting. Didn't like doing that but they understood when I told them about Serrano finding me. They've been so nice to me. I gave them my last week's pay and the pink slip to my old Honda to take care of the damages from the gunfight."

He wanted to reach out to her, drag her into his embrace and give her a big hug. Ten years in this business meant he knew how hard leaving friends and relatives behind could be on a witness—especially one that was innocent of any crime.

But he couldn't afford to show weakness right now. He needed to be the strong one. He needed to be the one who would save her and her son. And he would do that by going somewhere he had once sworn never to go again.

"I'll pay you back for that. I'm sorry…" He shut his mouth and turned his back so he couldn't see those eyes. "I've had an idea for a place we can hide out. But I need a phone. Did you find one anywhere?" Instead of fisting his hands, he polished off the orange juice.

"I used the motel office phone last night to call the neighbor and also my boss about our leaving the café open and shot up like that. But those were local calls. I don't think the manager will let you make a long distance call from there."

Figured. "How about your neighbor? The one taking care of Mikey. Think she'd let me use her phone if I left her plenty of money to take care of it?"

Sitting on the bed, to both keep his head from spinning and to jam his feet back into his boots, Sam glanced up at Grace.

She was staring down at him with an odd expression. "To tell the truth, I hadn't planned on sticking with you. I was going to insist you give me enough money to get out of town and then we'd split up. I have to think of Mikey."

His hands stilled with his foot in midair. "Grace, no. I swear…"

She held up her hands. "Don't worry. I've changed my mind. I know none of this is your fault."

Hesitating, her expression telegraphing depthless fear, she screwed up her mouth and then said on the next breath, "Mikey and I will go where you go. Do you need help with those boots?"

Seconds later he was standing on his booted feet and

looking for his coat. "No. Let's start moving. I need to run a couple of quick errands before we pick up the baby."

Quick errands? Sam hadn't been joking when he'd said "quick." In less than an hour they'd gone to a car dealership and traded in the old heap for a brand-new snazzy pickup with four doors and a full backseat.

He'd paid the difference in cash. She and the car dealer had both been stunned to see him dredge up a duffel full of currency and casually count out the money. It was all she could do to keep her mouth shut. That much cash could get a person in a lot of trouble.

Their next errand had been to the discount store to buy a car seat and a load of diapers for Mikey, some new jeans and a warm leather coat for her. Sam bought a couple of throwaway cell phones, tossed one in her direction and crammed the other in his coat pocket as they left the store.

While he drove them to her neighbor's house, she couldn't resist asking, "Why are you carrying so much cash? Aren't you worried about being robbed?"

That brought on a smile, but he didn't turn. "Being robbed is the last of my worries. I'm armed, remember? And using cash is the best way to disappear and leave no trace. Be grateful we're not trying to get away from Serrano's men on credit cards. Those records are too easy to trace if you know what you're doing."

"Wouldn't you need government assistance to obtain those kinds of records?"

"Theoretically. But computer hackers could bust into any system and retrieve all the info they want—without leaving a trace."

"Oh."

That information made her tremble. Sam had been

right. She didn't know nearly enough about how to disappear in a way to keep herself and her baby safe.

She needed him. At least for a while. But she was determined to pump him for information. Someday, she wouldn't need Sam Chance, or anyone else, to save her. She and Mikey could truly disappear on their own. They must find a place where Serrano's men would never find them. Never.

Sam parked the truck down the block from the neighbor's house. As they climbed out, Grace could hear sirens—and they seemed close.

Suddenly panicked, she started running toward the neighbor's house. *Mikey!*

"Grace, wait!"

She wasn't stopping for any reason. Mikey was her whole life. All she had left. Her life would be nothing without her baby.

Dashing straight down the quiet street to the neighbor's front door, she found the hidden key in the bush and barged right in. "Caroline? Mikey! Where are you?"

No answer.

Sam came through the door and shut it carefully behind him. "Any sign of a struggle?"

She ignored him and started for the kitchen.

"Careful, Grace." He pulled his gun and took her elbow to slow her down.

Grace was about to jerk her arm free and keep going when Caroline came around the corner carrying the baby in her arms. "You're here." Grace's knees went weak as she reached for her son.

Sam put his gun away and stepped behind her back, letting Grace lean against his chest for strength while she cradled Mikey.

"As you can see, Mikey's fine," Caroline said quietly. "But there's been trouble. I just got off the phone with Charlie. Apparently the desperados who are after you broke into your apartment over his garage, trashed it and set it on fire."

"Are Charlie and Mary okay?"

Caroline nodded and folded her arms across her stomach. "Scared to death—and worried about you two. They heard noises coming from the apartment after you'd left, so they sneaked out the back door. Called 9-1-1 from Charlie's cell, but the fire had already been set and the men long gone before the cops arrived."

Grace breathed deep of her son's baby powder and closed her eyes for a moment, so happy to have him in her arms that she could barely stand still. "I'm glad they're all right. Was the garage badly damaged?"

"Looks like it'll take a few thousand in repairs to put it right."

Crushed that she had been the cause of all this chaos, Grace vowed to find a way to pay them back.

"They need to stay away from their place for a few days. Maybe a week." Sam had been quiet all this time but now he stepped out from behind her in order to make his point.

Caroline looked him up and down then turned back to Grace. "This your U.S. Marshal? The one you mentioned?"

Not *her* Marshal. Though for a second Grace wished it could be true. No sense wishing for something that could never happen. She wasn't even sure she wanted *any* man—ever.

Sam stepped forward and stuck his hand out to Caroline. "U.S. Marshal Sam Chance, ma'am. Assigned to the WITSEC Program. Miss Grace and her son are under my protection."

Caroline thought about it a moment and then shook his hand. But as she did, she said, "Figure Grace was doing better on her own, son. No offense, but she don't seem all that safe with you."

Grace bit back a chuckle, jiggled Mikey in her arms—

And kept her mouth shut.

"No, ma'am. But I aim to right that situation from here on out. In the meantime, your neighbors need to move away from home for a while."

"That's what the police told them, too. They're going over to Abilene to visit Mary's sister for a week or two. Just till the café and the apartment can be repaired."

"Oh, look at all the trouble I've caused." Grace's heart twisted at the thought of everything her kind friends were going through because of her. "I'm so sorry. I…"

Caroline came closer and put her arm around her shoulders. "Never mind, honey. This ain't none of your doing and we know it. This here lawman didn't search you out to arrest you. He's here to protect you.

"Besides that," Caroline went on, while hugging her and Mikey close. "We know you. It don't matter what's behind all that's going on here. No one could convince me you'd done one blessed thing to bring any of this on yourself."

Mikey reached out his arms and clung to Caroline's neck. Grace felt the same way. She hated leaving these wonderful people behind.

Suddenly she knew what must've propelled Sam to her rescue. The obsessive need to protect a friend. And the only way for her to do that was to leave town and never look back.

"I'm afraid we have to go now, Caroline. Maybe you should leave for a few days, too."

Caroline took a half step back and picked up the baby's diaper bag. "Maybe I'll do just that. Been meaning to take a shopping trip to San Antonio for a long while now."

Grace turned and handed the baby over to Sam's care. Mikey's eyes widened and his face puckered up for a few seconds. But when he realized whose arms held him, the baby collapsed against Sam's broad chest and stuck his thumb in his mouth.

Grace pulled Caroline close for a full-out hug. "I appreciate all you've done. I can never thank…" The words choked her with emotion.

"Now, honey. I know how you feel. Charlie and Mary, too. We just wish there was something more we could do for you and the baby."

Caroline sighed and stepped away, handing over the bag. "Don't tell me where y'all are going. I don't want to know. But be safe." She turned to face Sam. "You'd just better keep her safe, son. Or you answer to me."

"Yes, ma'am. I'll protect both of them with my life."

Nodding sharply, Caroline sniffed and tilted her head toward the door. "Go on with you, then. And drive carefully."

As they made their way back to the new truck, Grace couldn't keep the tears from welling up in her eyes. She used her free hand to swipe them off her cheeks.

"Don't worry," Sam said quietly. "I'll send your boss a little more cash to make things right when we get where we're going. They'll be okay. It should take Serrano's men a few days to figure out you and the baby have left town for good. And I'll call the sheriff and have him keep an eye on your friends' places in the meantime."

"Thank you, Sam. That makes me feel a little better." But the tears wouldn't stop clouding her eyes.

"You all right?" Sam pulled the keys from his jacket pocket and unlocked the door.

She didn't answer him but simply shrugged her shoulders. Grace wasn't sure she would ever be really okay again.

But she had Mikey. That's all that mattered.

"Where are we going from here?" she asked as the two of them strapped Mikey into his seat in the back.

"If you'll drive us out of town, I need to make a phone call to double-check something. There shouldn't be any problem, but I need to tell them I'm coming."

"Tell who?"

"Just drive. I'll let you know where we're going after I make my call."

Well, she'd already decided to trust him with their lives. Even if her stomach rolled at the idea. Still, if she trusted him that much, she should turn over at least a little of the control—for a while.

But ohmygod, was that really the right thing to do?

Chapter 4

"Keep driving east on I-10," Sam told Grace. "We can cut north at Ozona."

The baby apparently hadn't wanted to leave Caroline behind. He'd cried and shrieked while they buckled him in his new car seat. Sam didn't suppose the boy's mother was any too happy about leaving her dear friend, either. Grace had been silent and thoughtful for the past fifteen minutes.

It had taken Sam most of that time to settle Mikey down. Finally, with his teething ring in his mouth and the steady sound of wheels against the pavement, Mikey's eyes fell closed and he was snoozing peacefully.

"We're staying in Texas?" Grace's voice held a note of terror. "Do you think that's smart? Who knows how many people Serrano has bought off in this part of the country."

"*You* came to Texas, didn't you?"

"I was planning on traveling through. If I hadn't run into Charlie and Mary, I would've been in Florida or New York by now." She swallowed hard. "Besides, I wanted a place where people speak my mother's language. I want Mikey to grow up knowing Spanish."

"That's also his father's language."

Grace shot him a narrowed look, but quickly returned her attention to driving.

No, he hadn't wanted to push her buttons. It was just an observation. But he promised himself from here on out to keep his mouth closed on that subject until Grace wanted to talk.

"Let me make this call," he said to break the icy silence. "If everything's okay, we're going to a place where Serrano can't have anyone in his pocket. Trust me."

She bit down on her lip but nodded her head.

Sam dialed a number he hadn't thought of in more years than he could count. But the digits came to mind easily.

A familiar voice answered the call. "Bar-C."

He pushed aside the heap of memories, both good and bad, assaulting his mind with that one word. "Hello, Travis. It's me."

"Sam." Not a question. Sam had known Travis would never forget his voice. "It's been too long, big brother. Is everything all right?"

The last time the two brothers had spoken it was Travis letting him know their father had been killed while in prison. Not exactly the best of memories. But one that stayed buried with all the other nasty recollections in the back of his mind.

"I'm okay. Everyone all right there?"

"Things are about the same here. Why are you calling, Sam?"

"I need a favor. I need a place to hide out for a while. Maybe quite some time, actually."

"Hide out? You change sides in the past few years?"

"I'm still a U.S. Marshal, Travis." His brother was a hell of a joker. "In fact, I have a witness and her child with me. But I need you to keep that information quiet."

Travis snorted through their connection. "You mean the WITSEC Program has run out of safe houses? What're our government bureaucracies coming to?"

"Not amused, brother. I'll tell you all about it when I see you. Can you make room for us or not?"

The tone of Travis's voice changed immediately. "Of course. The old homestead house has been sitting vacant since the rest of us moved out after Dad's death. That isolated enough for you?"

Sam seldom thought about the house where he grew up as isolated. But compared to the rest of the ranch, it certainly was.

"Then you actually built that new big ranch house and office space that you were talking about after Dad died?"

"It's been ten years now, Sam. Not so new anymore. Stop here on your way in. I'll show you around and feed you while a few of the hands get the old house cleaned up and stocked."

"We'll be there in a couple of hours. Okay?"

"Okay." Travis hesitated a second and Sam could hear his younger brother deciding what to say through the silence. "I'm glad you're headed home, Sam. It's been a long time. I've missed you."

A lump formed in Sam's throat but he gritted his

teeth and swallowed it back. Damn, but this trip down memory lane was going to take him through certain hell.

"Thanks for everything, Travis. See you in a little while." He hung up before his voice could crack.

Out of the corner of her eye Grace watched Sam sit quietly and stare at the phone that he continued to hold in his hand. A good five minutes after he'd said good-bye, he hadn't moved an inch. The conversation with his brother had obviously unnerved him.

Taking another glance out the back window like Sam had trained her to do, she found the same mostly empty stretch of rain-soaked highway that they'd just passed. No cartel vehicles seemed to be following. Hopefully they had gotten out of town without being spotted by Serrano's men. Things looked good so far. But she wasn't willing to let her guard down yet.

Deciding to break the silence, she cracked, "You have a family? No kidding. And here I always thought you must've come into this world fully formed. Guns, cowboy hat and all."

Sam shook his head and finally put the phone away. "Heh heh. Very funny. You're going to get along real well with my brothers. They're big jokers, too."

"I didn't know you were from this part of the country. You never mentioned growing up in Texas."

That did bring a smile to his face. "Talking to witnesses about your distant past isn't part of the job description. Didn't you have enough on your mind already?"

Grace kept a watchful eye out the windshield. Steady rain began turning to sleet and she needed a tighter grip on the wheel.

She hadn't cared for how Sam had put his last statement. She'd always imagined that the two of them were on their way to becoming good friends. At least until one of Serrano's men had shown up in Denver and scared her into running.

Of course she hadn't exactly spilled her guts about her past life to him, either. But Sam already knew most of the bad parts. Just not the ones that really mattered.

"You're frowning. Are you tired? The roads are icing. You want me to drive?"

She shook her head. "I'm fine. Not tired at all. But I want to know more about where we're going. And why you are so sure Serrano won't already have men there."

Sam sighed and pulled the cowboy hat lower on his forehead. "Not crazy about telling tales on myself. But I guess you'll hear it all soon anyhow."

His shoulders went up as though to protect him from the words he was about to speak. "I was born and raised on a Texas ranch and that's where we're headed. It's located in a pretty isolated county where everyone knows everybody else and Serrano's gang wouldn't stand a chance of setting up shop there. What else do you want to know?"

"When did you leave?"

"At nineteen. I joined the army."

Geez, couldn't he manage to string together more than four words at a time? Now he was making her curious.

"You said you had brothers. How many? And do they all still live there?"

He stayed quiet so long she had to sneak a glance to see if he'd fallen asleep. She'd never seen the man looking so pale. Even last night when he'd lost a lot of blood, he hadn't seemed so shaky and white. Like he'd seen a ghost.

"My mother had five boys and one girl. She and my dad are both gone now." The words were spoken quickly, as though he'd needed to expel them before they choked him.

"That's not a good enough answer, Sam. I want names, ages and places of residence for siblings, please." It was like pulling deep-rooted weeds to get this man talking.

"I'm the oldest. Just spoke to Travis, the next in line. He runs the ranch now. You'll be meeting him when we get there. Gage and Colt are both probably living either on the ranch or nearby. My…" He drew a breath, continued. "Youngest brother, named Denton, was killed in a ranching accident when he was eleven. And Cami—"

"Your sister? What happened to her?"

Sam cleared his throat. "She was…um…kidnapped. Right after our mother died. Cami was four at the time and Mom's sister said she'd better take her in for a while 'cause none of us boys would know what to do with a little girl. We all thought that sounded about right. We were teenage boys who were on our own, and she was supposedly our loving auntie.

"Trouble was…" he went on slowly. "My mother's sister, Sally, was a junkie and we didn't know it. She took Cami and disappeared."

"Oh, my gosh. Didn't the FBI look for her?"

Sam sat a little straighter. "Of course they did. The Bureau tracked my aunt all the way to L.A. Then they lost her. Next time my aunt Sally showed up was in a San Diego morgue five years later. Overdosed."

Grace took a deep breath. "And they never found your little sister," she said in a whisper, "I'm so sorry."

Yes, she was sorry. Both for his family losses and his

obvious misery. But she was also sorry she'd pushed him to tell the story.

"I'd heard that my brother Gage started a P.I. firm a few years back. I expect they've done everything they can to find her themselves. But it's tough after all these years to get a lead on one little girl."

The way he'd said that sounded to Grace as if he had done some looking himself. Without much luck. The poor man. Her heart twisted for Sam and his brothers.

Then her mind got stuck on something else he'd said. "What did you mean that you'd *heard* about the P.I. firm? Don't you know for sure?"

"Haven't talked to any of my brothers in the past ten years or so."

Then he hadn't left on good terms with his family? Now Grace was becoming more curious than ever. Every time he gave her one piece of information, it brought up more questions. This was a complicated man.

"But you have been keeping tabs on them. From a distance." Otherwise how would he know about the P.I. firm?

"Some." Sam pushed his hat back. "We're coming up to the turnoff. Pull into a gas station and I'll drive the rest of the way in."

Grace was ready to stretch her legs and Mikey needed a diaper change. So she pulled in to the pumps at a truck stop. Twenty minutes later they were on their way again.

Sam drove down a country road as the sleet turned back into drizzle. After getting Mikey resettled in the car seat with a bottle, she glanced over to check on Sam. His mouth was set so hard the jawline looked as if it would cut diamonds.

She didn't imagine she would get much more out of

him for now. Relaxing back in her seat, she stared out the window at the passing scenery.

Still stuck in late winter cold, the famous Texas wildflowers were nowhere to be seen alongside the roads. But the dry, rocky country they'd just left around Fort Stockton had given way to miles and miles of flat fields, punctuated by a nice river and a couple of gullies here and there. Bare cottonwood trees grew in the gullies, alongside what she thought were mesquite and dark green juniper trees. Off in the distance tall mesas and cliffs loomed in the background. The whole vista looked a lot like a landscape painting.

"Seems like excellent grazing land."

"Good guess. You ever been on a working ranch before?"

"No. Never. But I've seen them in movies."

That brought the first smile to Sam's face since she'd asked about his family. She loved seeing him smile. It brightened his whole demeanor.

Suddenly it occurred to her what she hadn't seen. Not since they'd left the truck stop. Houses. Stores. Gas stations. In fact, there hadn't been one indication of human life in the past hour.

As the afternoon shadows grew long, Grace began to feel more and more isolated. She checked on Mikey more than once. But the baby had fallen back to sleep and seemed oblivious to his mother's worries.

Another half hour went by and still nothing but bleak country and cold rain. Not even as much as a road sign. The skin on her arms began to crawl.

She was about to tell Sam to turn around and go back, that they must've taken a wrong turn, when they rounded a curve and the first sign of civilization popped into view—in the form of an actual signpost. The sign read: Welcome to Chance—Population: 826.

"Chance? There's a town named Chance?"

"Yep. Been here since my great-great-granddaddy arrived in 1886. Right after the railroad was finished and the army abandoned the nearest fort."

"Your family founded the town?" Just think of that.

"Well, it wasn't much back then. Still isn't by the looks of things."

Grace stared up at an old service station and across from that a big barn of a building with a sign that said it was the Feed and Seed Store. Driving on down what seemed to be the main street in town, she saw a café and a string of small businesses. Beauty and barber shops, a hardware store, and insurance agent and a medium-size bank.

Everything looked old but spotless. Well maintained.

"Well, this looks nice," she mumbled. "How much farther to your home?"

"Only about a half hour now."

"Another half hour? How is that possible?"

"Distances are long in Texas."

"Yes, but this is the town of Chance. Surely your family's ranch should be right around here someplace close."

"Real close. We've been on my family's ranch for about the past twenty miles or so. Most of the land around here belongs to the Bar-C. Except for the town proper, of course."

Stunned, Grace sat back and stared out the window as they passed through the town and kept on driving. The miles rolled by in a blur of country road, driving rain and empty land. Good Lord, his family must be worth millions.

Just who was this man who'd come to save her?

Chapter 5

Sam prepared to turn at the ranch-to-market road that led to the main gate. The rain had turned to drizzle and he got his first real glimpse of the land where he'd grown up.

Memories tumbled from some deep arroyo in his mind. Of riding his horse across the field after a foot of snowfall—unusual for this part of Texas. And of chasing his junior high sweetheart into that stock pond one spectacular and starry spring night for his first kiss.

All good memories. He remembered the exhilaration of being young.

That was long before his mother died and his father was sent to prison. In fact, the only things to mar the sweet recollections of his budding adolescence were the memories of a too-stern father. The father that had made outrageous demands on his oldest son.

"You will take over the ranch someday," his father

had insisted. "You'll run it with an iron fist, the same as your grandfather Samuel. You're the oldest. Named for a great man. It's your destiny."

But Sam hadn't wanted to run the ranch. Oh, he loved his family and liked the land and the animals well enough. But Sam had wanted to travel. See the world. Besides, back then he'd been much better at taking orders than dishing them out. Why couldn't his father ever see that?

Turning right toward the gate, Sam absently drove the pickup over the old cattle guard and the whole truck shook. He'd forgotten how loud a cattle guard could sound under the tires of a big vehicle.

"What the heck was that?" Grace sat straight up. Then she turned to check on Mikey, who'd been jolted awake by the noise and now was screaming at the top of his lungs.

"Sorry. It's just…" At that moment he spied the Bar-C fence and gate. Twenty-foot-high metalwork loomed across the road about sixty feet ahead.

"Holy moly. Is this place for real?" Grace had spotted it, too. "Look at that. The gate is huge. And spectacular looking. I'd bet the scrollwork on that Bar-C at the top gleams like pure gold in the bright sunlight."

"Hmm. Maybe. The gate's new." And they would have to stop and use the call box in order to enter. "When I was a kid, we'd climb out of the truck and open the gate ourselves. Things have changed."

"I guess." The smile in Grace's voice, the first in a long while, didn't do much to soothe his irritation at the changes to his old homestead.

But then, what did he expect? He'd changed a lot in the past fifteen years since he had left home. Why shouldn't the ranch change, as well?

He tried to keep an open mind as he punched the call button and gained entry. The gate swung open as if all by itself and Sam gritted his teeth while driving through.

In a few moments he drove past enormous barn-like structures and spotted animal pens in the distance packed with cattle being sheltered and fed while they waited for the spring market. The whole scene looked prosperous and modern.

Way to go, Travis. His brother had done a terrific job of running the ranch. And once Sam had that thought, he relaxed and began cataloging all the new things he should congratulate his brother for accomplishing.

Looked like the right person had inherited the boss's job after all.

Within a half mile they passed what looked like an indoor horse ring. A single-story structure in front of the ring held a sign that said: Bar-C Executive Offices.

"This is amazing," Grace said as they drove on by. "I bet not all ranches look like this one."

Not even close. In another moment Sam spotted a two-story mansion that looked like something from one of those old eighties TV dramas set in Texas. This house was where the family lived now?

Sam drove up the wide circular drive and stopped in front of the huge double-door entry. "Well, I guess this is my brother's house."

"I'll get Mikey out of his car seat if you'll grab his diaper bag."

"Sure." Popping the seat belt, Sam turned to step out of the truck's cab.

Before he could step down, though, the double doors opened and his brother strode down the steps, heading in his direction. "Sam."

Coming around the hood, Sam stuck out his hand to Travis. But his brother apparently had other ideas, pulling him into a bear hug.

Enveloped in the warmth of his brother's embrace, Sam felt both guilt and a deep sadness running up his spine. Those feelings and a twinge in his shoulder disturbed him enough to step back.

"Are you injured?" Travis nodded his head toward Sam's arm

"Naw. It's only a scratch."

Travis's smile was as melancholy as Sam felt. "It's been too long, damn it, bubba."

Sam had to smile at his brother's use of his childhood nickname. And he was surprised by how strong and genuine his emotions ran.

"This is some place you've built, Trav. Good work."

His brother's lips tipped up in a half-smile and he opened his mouth to make another remark. But right then something happened that Sam had never counted on. And the tiny voice made even Travis fall silent and turn.

"Daddy? Who's out here?"

Grace looked up at the sound of a little girl coming down the front stoop of the enormous house. The child appeared to be about eight or nine, blond with long pigtails and dressed in jeans and cowboy boots.

Sam hadn't mentioned his brother having children. But this child must certainly belong to his younger brother. Even if the girl hadn't called him daddy, and except for their hair coloring, the resemblance was unmistakable.

Right down to the air of confidence and the everyone-must-do-as-I-say attitude.

"Jenna. Where's your coat? Stay inside. We'll be there in a minute."

Travis's voice could've been heard at least a half mile away but the girl acted as if she'd never heard a word. Coming down the steps, she stood toe-to-toe with Sam.

The tiny person craned her neck to look him up and down, then after a moment she said, "You must be my uncle Sam. The one that ran away."

Sam's expression quickly turned from surprise to something like sorrow. Grace would've loved to have taken him in her arms and begged him to tell her the whole story. Why he'd left this magical place and stayed away for so long. As much as she was beginning to trust him with her and Mikey's safety, there was something going on inside this man and she wanted to know what.

He managed to hide his emotions when he said, "Yes, ma'am. That would be me. And how old are you, niece Jenna?"

Instead of answering the question, which apparently bored her, Jenna turned to stare at the other strangers getting out of the truck. "A baby! Oh, Daddy, you didn't tell me a *baby* was coming to the Bar-C."

She flew over to where Grace was standing by the pickup. "Is it a boy or a girl?"

"Jenna! Inside right now!" Travis's voice had taken a much sterner tone.

Still Jenna continued to ignore her father.

She raised her arms and gave Grace a pleading smile. "Can I hold the baby?"

Out of the corner of her eye Grace could see Travis heading their way, and he did not look happy. She suddenly took pity on the little girl.

"This is Mikey," she told Jenna. "And he's probably

too heavy for you to hold. But you can show us inside the house so he doesn't catch cold out here."

Grace knew her son was bundled up and in no danger of being cold. But she hoped what she'd said would move the little girl inside before her father had time to reach them.

"Oh, sure. Come on in." Jenna spun and marched straight for the front door, totally ignoring the other adults who were now standing like statues, staring silently at the oblivious little girl.

Grace couldn't help smiling at the sight of those blond pigtails bouncing up the steps. She supposed she'd been a lot like Jenna at that age. Except not blond, of course. But so sure of herself. So sure that everyone in her world loved her unconditionally. Grace remembered thinking she could get away with anything. Do whatever she pleased and still be loved.

Too bad reality always intrudes on life.

Glancing over at Travis and Sam, Grace said, "It's okay for us to go inside, isn't it?"

Travis looked chagrined. "Of course. Sorry…Mrs.…."

Sam stepped between his brother and Grace. "Trav, this is Grace Baker and her son, Mikey. We can make proper introductions later if that's okay with you."

Grabbing Mikey's diaper bag out of the pickup and then slamming the doors, Sam stepped it up so he could reach for her elbow and helped her negotiate the slippery steps while carrying the baby. Jenna held the front door wide-open and practically grabbed hold of Grace's coattails as she passed by. The little girl shadowed her as they entered the wide foyer.

"This is my house," Jenna said, beaming up at Mikey. "It's nice and warm in here."

Once again Grace thought of herself at that age. *So sure. So sure.*

At that moment three huge dogs came sliding around a corner on the hardwood floors. Two black long-haired breeds and one reddish-colored, short-haired dog, they were all over a hundred pounds apiece, panting hard and racing toward Jenna. Grace backed up to lean against Sam, fearful of the dogs jumping up and knocking into the baby.

Travis's commanding voice came from right behind her. "Jenna, take the dogs outside. Now."

As if coming out of a dream, Jenna's expression said she'd suddenly realized a huge catastrophe could happen at any moment. She began moving toward the dogs. Using a commanding voice of her own, she stopped them in their tracks. In moments all four of them, three dogs and one tough little girl, disappeared around the same corner where the animals had first entered the room.

"Sorry about that. That child will be the death of her old man yet." Travis moved into the lead. "Let's go where we can talk. Maybe have some coffee?"

Grace started to follow Sam and Travis but just then Mikey began to fuss. She knew immediately what was wrong.

"Uh. Is there someplace where I can change Mikey first?"

"Sure." Travis turned and hollered, "Jenna!"

Before he could even shut his mouth again, his daughter was right beside him. "Yes, Daddy?"

"Take Ms. Baker and the baby upstairs and show them the blue guest room. She needs to change his diaper. Stay with them and then bring her back downstairs to the great room when they're finished."

Grace turned to Jenna. "Can you carry Mikey's bag?"

"Sure I can." Jenna took the diaper bag from Sam and trundled toward the stairs. "Can I help change the baby?"

"We'll see." Hmm. This was turning into an interesting and unique experience for all of them.

Sam watched Grace negotiate the stairs, following his niece. *His niece.* Why hadn't he known about Jenna? And where was Travis's wife? Had he been living his isolated life for so long, sheltering one witness after another, that he'd totally lost track of his family?

His growing family.

Following his brother into a room that looked more like a hunting lodge than a *Dallas* mansion, Sam's shoulders began to relax. A big fire roared in the oversize stone fireplace and the leather sofas and gleaming wood tables actually made a fairly comfortable place for a family get-together.

The only thing seeming out of place was the feeling that in the entire room there wasn't one item that looked the least bit like it had been placed there by the hand of a woman. So where was Jenna's mama?

First question he wanted to ask.

Travis offered him a seat and a cup of coffee. "Rosie the housekeeper is making us an early supper. But I thought you might like a beer instead of coffee."

Sam shook his head as he shrugged out of his jacket. The shoulder was still tender and Travis caught him wincing.

"All right, give. What'd you do to the arm?"

"Long story. Bullet grazed me last night. But it's healing fine."

"You want Doc to come out and take a look?"

"No. Thanks. But I will take a cup of coffee if you're still offering." Sam sat on the leather sofa and glanced around the room. "You've really got some place here. Fancy new house. And the Bar-C operation looks prosperous. You even hired a housekeeper instead of just using one of the hands to do the cooking. I'm impressed."

Travis handed him a strong, black steaming cup of coffee. "The housekeeper is mainly for Jenna. And the ranch is doing okay. Which you would know if you'd talked to the accountants once in a while. You still own a fifth of the ranch and are welcome to look at the books anytime. But you haven't had any questions in ten years. What is it you're really asking, Sam?"

Yeah, his brother was sure to guess that Sam was gearing up for a question and answer session. Travis had always been able to read him—too well.

"It's nothing to do with the ranch or the money," Sam said quietly. "It's no trick to see you've done a terrific job growing the Bar-C into a world-class operation. And I did contact the accountants a few weeks ago to withdraw some money from my trust. The ranch's cash flow is probably okay or I would've heard about it."

"So?" Travis sat on the edge of a chair and leaned against his elbows against his knees.

"So…how come I don't know about your daughter? The last time we talked you were considering marrying your old sweetheart from high school, Callie Jones. My guess is you did. Why didn't you call to let me know you're a dad and I'm an uncle?"

The way Travis shrugged a shoulder told Sam a lot, but not enough. "Is Callie Jenna's mother? And where is she?"

"Sam, you left us, not the other way around. It hasn't

always been easy reaching you with chatty news items. Callie is Jenna's mom." Travis stood again and stretched. "Though I suspect Callie would rather you not spread that around. We were married about ten years ago, had Jenna right away and, by the time our daughter was six months old, Callie was long gone."

"Gone where?"

"Nashville. Following her dream." Travis turned to the small refrigerator in the bar, opened it and waved a long-necked bottle in Sam's direction. "Sure I can't tempt you with one of these?"

Sam shook his head, but almost relented. He suddenly felt in need of something stronger than coffee after hearing how his brother and niece had been dumped by a girl he remembered as every high school jock's dream date.

But Travis didn't seem ready to talk about himself. He sank low in one of the barrel chairs and took a long slug from the beer bottle.

Sam knew he would get answers sooner or later. He knew his brother well enough to find out what he needed. But he decided later would be better.

"Before Grace comes back downstairs, I need to tell you a little about her background. You have the right to know who you're harboring."

Travis's eyebrows shot up. "Don't tell me she's an axe murderer disguised as a mother."

Refusing to give up a smile, Sam didn't dignify the joke with a comment. "She was a federal witness against one of Mexico's biggest drug lords. Jose Serrano. His gang's been making inroads into U.S. territory for years. Grace's testimony convicted him in U.S. court in absentia. If the Marshals can recapture him and put him back in custody, he'll do three life terms."

"I've heard about Serrano. Nasty piece of work. Isn't he the one who's murdered several federal agents? His operation is supposed to be mostly along the California and Arizona borders."

"Don't count on it. He could be branching out all along the U.S. border. You should know there might be danger if we stay on the ranch."

Travis looked thoughtful. "What kind of testimony could one single mother possibly provide that would sentence such a powerful bad guy to prison for three life terms?"

Sam figured his brother was wondering if Grace had been part of the gang—or perhaps Serrano's lover. The last option was only partly true and Sam wanted to set Travis straight.

"Serrano kidnapped Grace when she was just nineteen. The kidnapping was a ploy to force her father to stop writing editorials in his San Diego Spanish-language newspaper about Serrano and his operation."

Waiting for the rest, Travis set his beer down and narrowed his eyes as he focused on Sam's face. "Go on."

"While he waited for an answer from her father, the damned drug lord decided a beautiful young virgin was just too choice to pass up. He raped her and then forced her to become his lover, using a combination of drugs and physical coercion."

"How long did Serrano hold her captive?"

"Nearly four years."

"What? But…"

"Yeah, he'd threatened to kill her if her father didn't comply with his demands. But when Grace's father stood on principle and went to the FBI for help instead of giving in, Serrano retaliated by killing both Grace's parents and destroying their newspaper offices in a massive explosion."

Sam stopped to release a pent-up breath. "Bastard decided he would keep Grace for himself as a sort of consolation prize."

"Oh, my God. How'd she ever live through such an ordeal and get away?"

Sam could hear noises on the stairwell and knew Grace was on her way down with both kids in tow. "Another long story. Suffice to say, Grace Baker is one smart lady. She's…she's…" He'd started to say *strong* or maybe he would've said *vital,* but the words stuck in his throat.

He couldn't really say how he felt about Grace—except that he was determined to save her life. And he didn't want to think much about it for now, either.

His brother turned his head to the voices coming their way, but swung back to whisper, "I get it. And the baby?"

Travis's expression seemed to suggest he thought something more personal was going on between them. Yes, there had been times when Sam had wished both Grace and Mikey belonged to him, but they didn't. And they never would.

"Nothing's going on between me and Grace, Trav. It's my duty to save both her and her son from Mikey's father. That's all."

And he swore he would. Or die trying.

Chapter 6

Frustrated, Jose Serrano turned his back on his own mother, clenched his fists and stormed into the office.

Slamming the door shut with such force it could be felt throughout the entire hacienda, Jose glared at his two *empleados* as they jumped up from their seats.

"My mother is not pleased," he grumbled in Spanish. "She'd hoped to hold her grandson for the first time today, and did not care to hear the news that you'd failed."

Both men's eyes grew wide in terror, but neither one had the balls to speak. All right, he knew failing to capture his son alive and well was not entirely their fault. These men were trained in mass chaos. For the most part he only employed murderers and criminals. That type would, of course, have trouble using gentle tactics designed to capture a baby.

Brains. He needed someone who had enough intelligence to accomplish the job without bloodshed.

Slumping into his massive desk chair and waving the men out of the room, much to their relief, Jose wondered how his life had grown so out of control. He hated being confined here in Mexico. Even if this house of his confinement was the most luxurious place money could buy. He'd built it a few years back for his mother. But it had never made her particularly happy.

His mother wanted grandchildren. Most especially she wanted a grandson. Someone to carry on the family name.

But Jose had been a little too busy building his empire to stop and find a nice woman. A woman pure enough to carry his seed and his name.

Finding such a woman had been both a pleasant surprise and a blessing he had not counted on. Shifting in his seat as he thought of the beautiful woman who had shared his bed, Jose hated to admit that he missed her.

She had brains to go along with her phenomenal body. Who would've thought that he could find such a gem of a woman in the guise of a nineteen-year-old college student?

The woman who now called herself Grace Baker would be able to come up with a plan to take a nearly one-year-old child without force.

Unfortunately he no longer could count on her council—or on the blessed relief of her body at the day's end. Her supreme treachery still grated on his nerves and he would probably kill her for it in the end. The word could not go out that a snitch could turn Jose Serrano in and live. It wouldn't be good for morale.

But first he wanted his son to come home. And he wanted that word out on the streets almost as much as he wanted Grace to suffer. Jose Serrano was a man's man. *He* could father a son.

Staring blankly at the blinking computer screen in front of him, he tried not to think of his current business problems. He needed to come up with a new plan to find Grace and the baby and then capture them alive. That gringo lawman, who'd spirited them out of Fort Stockton, was a smart man. A man to match wits against.

But Jose was just as smart. If only he wasn't currently embroiled in ugly skirmishes with several rival gangs along the border. None of those rival *estúpidos* would've had the nerve to challenge the Serrano gang's superiority and firepower had it not been for his own embarrassment of having to flee the U.S. from a jail cell.

The men he had left in charge of his business interests in California were losing control. And he would have to do something soon to remedy that situation.

But first he needed to locate Grace and his son. There was one man he could approach for help. The man who had helped him in the past and had given his men the means to follow Grace before.

Jose's gut feeling was that the lawman who had snatched her just as his men arrived would again be the key to finding them. That lawman thought like Jose. Clever. He would conceal them in a place where no one would think to look.

If he was trying to hide someone, Jose imagined he might bring her into Mexico. The last place anyone would look. But no, this lawman was *americano*. He would not cross borders where he could not count on friendly assistance from other lawmen.

So where else would someone clever go? Back to Los Angeles? Perhaps. Back to the scene of Grace's betrayal.

No, shaking his head, Jose didn't think that fit the man, either.

But at last he had a spark of an idea. He picked up the phone and placed a call.

The man he wanted answered after the first ring. "I need your services again."

"Very well. But we will renegotiate terms. You must realize my position is precarious and I need more funds to make it worth my while."

Jose had figured something like this would be coming. But after all, the man's greed was what had allowed Jose to turn him to his own purposes in the beginning. And greed would keep this two-faced man working and silent, for now.

"Double your last fee," Jose told him. "But you only receive half as down payment. You will find the other half in your bank account when my son is safe in my home."

The man sought to argue terms but he was smart enough to hear the determination—and the implied threat—in Jose's tone. Negotiations ended before they truly began.

"What do you need now?"

"That Marshal," Jose said in a steady voice. "The one who's gone rogue in order to keep my son and his mother from their rightful destiny with me. I want his background. I want to know everything there is to know about this gringo."

"I can supply his file."

"Not enough. I want more. I want it all." Jose knew that somewhere in the lawman's background he would find the one thing that would give him a clue to where such a man would go to feel safe.

Because there was nowhere he would truly be out of Jose Serrano's reach. Nowhere at all.

Chapter 7

Grace slipped a sleepy Mikey into his car seat in the back of the pickup. It had been a long day and, though the baby had been thrilled to find a playmate in Jenna, he was now exhausted and cranky.

Grace felt drained, too.

Sam stood a few feet away talking softly to his brother. The rain had stopped and the temperature was dropping. An icy haze surrounded the two men and each word exited on a puffy breath.

She caught a little of what they were saying, even from this distance.

"You want me to send a few men to guard the old homestead while you're there?" Travis reached out a hand to grab his brother's shoulder.

Sam shook his head and eased back. "Naw. I can keep them safe. Your men have their own jobs to do. This one is mine. Besides, I don't think Serrano will find us here. That's why we came."

"Don't get too complacent, bubba. Like I said, Serrano is a nasty piece of work. Remember that. I intend to be a lot more watchful and keep checking backgrounds on anyone who enters the ranch."

Grace missed a few of the sentences that passed between the brothers while she quietly closed Mikey into the truck's backseat trying not to wake him, and then opened the front passenger door. As she climbed up into the seat, she turned her head for a moment and listened again.

Sam was saying, "Serrano may want Grace dead. That isn't clear. But there's no question from what happened back in Fort Stockton that his main goal is capturing his son alive."

His son. Jose's son. Grace slumped into the seat, closed the door and leaned her head against the window.

All her embarrassment came rushing back along with the chill north winds. She felt like such an idiot. How could she have given in to a drug lord?

Even having been a rather naive college girl when she'd been taken, she should never have believed anything an animal like Jose said. Men like him lied for a living. He was a mean-spirited criminal who'd kidnapped, abused and raped her. What would ever make her believe otherwise?

Above the guilty thoughts and solid regrets, Grace could hear Sam bidding good-night to his brother. She shoved her thoughts back to where they belonged. Somewhere so deep they couldn't reach her conscious mind. She'd worked hard to stop caring what other people said about her during the trial. Now she didn't have the energy left to be a good mother to her son and still fight the hurt of shameful words, too.

Oh, Dad, I'm sorry that I was weak. Maybe if I'd stayed strong...

"You two okay and ready to go?" Sam slid into the driver's seat and started the engine.

"We're set."

"Travis said he'd bring Jenna out for a visit as soon as we settle in. Hope that's all right."

"It's fine. I really liked your brother and his little girl. I feel sorry for them without a woman in their lives, and I appreciate getting a chance to hide out on their ranch."

Sam put the truck in gear. "The ranch belongs to the whole family. But yeah, Trav is a good guy."

Hesitating at the end of the circle driveway, Sam turned to her. "You look tired. This should only take about fifteen minutes. Rest. Don't worry about a thing. I'll get us there in one piece."

Suddenly she realized why her feelings for Sam kept running hot and cold. For the whole time she'd known him she'd gone from wanting to be his friend to wishing to become his lover, and then to being sure he was the enemy.

Now she knew why. He was too black and white. Too much like her father had been.

God, she was such an emotional wreck. The physical scars had healed long ago but the scars on her psyche were as deep as ever. Seeing Sam with his family had brought it all back.

And that's why she and Mikey would be better off on their own. Sam wouldn't get hurt if she was a thousand miles away, and she could bury her old traumas and make herself believe she was like any other normal single mother.

Yeah, right. What normal single mother was running from Mexico's biggest drug lord? Mikey would never know his father, not if she could help it. But he also would never know his grandparents. And maybe that was all her fault.

"I'd bet there's a crib in the attic. Let me get a flashlight and I'll check." Sam turned from the second-floor bedroom and disappeared down the hall.

Grace could barely keep her eyes open and Mikey was dead to the world, softly snoring on the wide bed in what used to be Sam's parents' old room. She sank down on the edge of the bed and forced her eyes to stay open.

This was a fascinating old farmhouse. And tomorrow she would go exploring the many different levels and rooms. But for tonight all she wanted to do was sleep. A deep, dreamless sleep where she wasn't being chased by a criminal and hadn't made the many mistakes of her past.

Trying to trick her brain into dwelling on anything else while waiting for Sam, she turned her thoughts to the man instead of on herself. Ever since his old family home had come into view out of the truck's windshield, he'd been acting a little odd. There'd been a strange look, something not quite right, in his eyes as he found the key over the door jamb and came inside.

Everything about the house had looked delightful to her. Cozy. Warm. Someone had made up the beds and even left a fire going in the downstairs fireplace. Knickknacks and kids' trophies adorned nearly every surface. Dim lighting made the rooms glow, like a real home should. Grace loved it immediately. She couldn't believe any family would walk away from this wonderful house.

But something about this place, or more likely about his childhood, had obviously left him conflicted. Maybe the good guy in the white hat she'd thought she'd known for the past six months was really a wounded soul deep down—the same as her. The idea was something to think about.

She felt a twinge of empathy. Then her curiosity overruled her better judgment.

Prying the entire truth from him might be a bad move, however. Sam thought he knew all about her. Thought he knew her whole story. But if she began to question him too closely about his inner demons, he might feel entitled to turn the tables on her.

And that wasn't going to happen.

The smell of coffee brewing drew Sam out of his sleep. But his aching shoulder and a roaring headache kept him sitting on the edge of the bed, groggy and in pain instead of getting up. Hell.

He glanced around, looking for his jeans, but his gaze landed on the familiar objects in the too-familiar room. He'd slept in his and Travis's old bedroom because there'd been more space for Mikey's crib in his parents' old room.

Now he wished he'd slept downstairs on the couch. Or not come back to this house at all.

Too many memories. Too many objects to remind him of his youth.

He'd spent the better part of the past fifteen years forgetting. Setting aside all the painful memories. But with one sweeping glance every one of them had come back in a raw and throbbing rush.

Well, no help for it. This was where he could keep Grace and Mikey the safest. Serrano's men had little chance of either finding or getting to them this far inside the ranch. So this was where they would stay.

Might as well get on with his job and the forced reminiscing. He absently rubbed at his aching shoulder a couple of times and stood. Painkillers would be in order before coffee.

Easing into a soft flannel shirt then pulling on his jeans and boots took some doing. But after a quick cleanup in the bathroom and downing two pills, he found himself feeling half decent as he rounded a downstairs corner into a kitchen that came right out of his childhood.

No one had changed a thing in all these years. His mother's wallpaper was still intact. His grandfather's handmade rough-hewn cabinets still hung at an uneven slant. It even smelled the same as he remembered.

"Good morning." Grace looked up from her spot at the table beside Mikey and grinned. A smile that reached her eyes. "Are you still in pain?"

"I'm fine. Just a little stiff. You made coffee."

She handed Mikey a quarter piece of toast and said, "Travis must've had someone stock food. The cabinets and the refrigerator are loaded. We could probably hide out here for a year and never see a soul."

Sam reached for a mug without thinking and his hand automatically landed on the one with the chip in the bottom that had always been his. "Don't count on it. Travis told me that the Bar-C is using the homestead's old barns, the ones my father built, for much of their horse breeding and foaling operations. The barns are located about a half mile down the lane, but the road out front is the only way of getting there."

Grace shrugged. "No one will stop here, will they?"

"I doubt it. Not too many people working on those operations at this time of year." He poured coffee and took a seat opposite Grace and the baby. "But I'd bet a month's pay that Jenna will show up just as soon as she can find a way past her father."

Laughing, Grace nodded. "She was pretty miffed about our leaving last night. That child really took to Mikey in a big way."

"I think she's lonely. Misses having a mama around."

Grace stood and said, "I made Mikey scrambled eggs for breakfast, you want some?"

"Coffee's fine."

"I remember being Jenna's age and wanting a baby brother or sister to play with—in the worst way." Grace tilted her head and looked Sam straight in the eye. "You need to eat something to get your strength back. It'll only take a moment."

As she turned the gas on under the burner she went on, "You said you grew up with a big family. I suppose you wouldn't know how it is to be an only child."

"No, I never…"

Just then Mikey interrupted the conversation by pitching his remaining toast directly at Sam's chest. Then with a big whoop and a toothy grin, he said, "Da!"

Grace ignored her son's outburst but Sam needed to take a deep breath as he unbuckled the baby from the family's old high chair. The moment turned into yet one more occasion when he wished he was this cute baby's daddy. But where were those thoughts coming from?

He'd tried for most of his life to keep away from the prospect of a wife and children of his own. Some of his close relatives, namely his father and grandfather, had been what people used to label "dysfunctional" and that was enough to make Sam hesitant to wish for a family of his own.

Yeah, Grace's kid was special in a lot of ways, and Sam would do anything to keep him safe. But he also figured that in the long haul living with a man like himself would be a curse on any child.

Shaking free of the sudden melancholy such thoughts brought on, he settled the baby in the crook of one arm and turned to Grace. "I haven't seen Mikey in weeks. His top teeth are all in. How many words can he say?"

Grace set a plate of eggs in front of him and gave him a look that said he had better eat. "A handful. Still not many. But he calls every man he sees *Da* or *Da Da.*"

She chuckled and went on, "Calls all the women *Ma* or *Mama,* too. Don't take it too much to heart. And put him down on the floor now so you can eat. Floor's so clean you could use it as a plate. He'll be fine."

"Does he walk already?" Sam gently placed Mikey in a sitting position on the floor beside his chair.

But Mikey quickly toppled himself over and began to crawl. He disappeared under the table so fast that in a moment Sam lost track of him.

"Uh…" Grace looked down at her leg as Mikey appeared, pulling himself up into a standing position against her by using her jeans as a handhold. "Not by himself yet. But obviously he's standing alone, and Caroline told me he's been cruising around holding on to the furniture, too. It won't take him long."

Sam shoveled the eggs into his mouth. He knew he would never get away from the table without eating first. Grace was a very determined woman.

And he very much needed to get away from this table. The scene was too intimate. Too cozy. He needed air.

Popping the last bite into his mouth and pushing himself back, he told her, "I think I'll take a walk around the property and down to the barn. See what things look like after all these years."

"Oh, can we go, too? Will it be safe for us outside? No one could, um, shoot at us from a distance or anything?"

Damn near swallowing his tongue, Sam managed to speak. "It's safe enough outside. But are you sure you…"

"We'd love a walk. Let me just bundle Mikey up and put on his shoes."

"Grace, the barns are quite a distance for a baby and it's cold. Why do you want to go?"

She lifted Mikey in her arms and headed toward the stairs. "It'll give you and me a good opportunity to talk. I want to hear all about your childhood on the ranch."

Hell. He never talked to anyone about his childhood. He hadn't even mentioned his ranching background in his basic employee file for the Marshals. Not a chance he'd be spilling his guts to Grace, either.

Chapter 8

The air was crisp but not cold, the sky a cornflower blue. Sam walked his two charges down the one-lane road toward the barns, amazed the weather, as usual in West Texas, had made a complete one-eighty turn from last night.

While their little group was circling around the house and grounds, he'd noticed quite a few projects that needed attending. Thinking they might make good excuses for him to stay out of the house while stuck here on the ranch with Grace and the baby, he mentally prepared a list of supplies he would need.

Grace remained mostly quiet, only making a comment now and then or softly murmuring to Mikey, safely snuggled in her arms. Sam wondered when the interrogation would begin.

In the meantime he glanced around at their surroundings. At the fields and fences of his youth. He felt surprisingly safe. A condition he never allowed himself to feel. His job was to make other people feel secure when by all rights they should be scared and under their beds. Anytime he let down his guard long enough to feel protected in his surroundings might mean the end of everything.

Yet he couldn't help it this time. He'd grown up here and had always felt at ease on the Bar-C. It was hard to think that a goon like Serrano could be stalking him even on the ranch.

"Look, Mikey," Grace said aloud. "That's a river. And those are trees. Aren't they pretty?"

Not far in the distance, the North Concho was visible as it wound its way through the landscape.

"Most of those trees you're seeing are willows," he told Grace. "And a few pecans grow in the low spots. My mom used to bake pecan pies and she'd make us kids crack the nuts from those trees. Seemed like it used to take about a thousand per pie."

"Really? Tell me about your mom."

Now why the hell had he opened his big mouth? He would not discuss his mother. Her story hadn't ended well and Sam didn't want to remember. He hated thinking about her, to tell the truth.

"She was a regular mom. Did a decent job of raising six kids. Taught me how to make a bed, wash my own clothes and take orders. I appreciated having that knowledge in the army."

They'd arrived at the gate to the foaling barns. "Well, here we are. Want to get a little closer? See what we've got inside the barns?"

"Sure. I guess so." Grace shifted Mikey from one arm to the other.

Sam opened the gate and twisted back to them.

"Here, let me carry the baby for a while. Wouldn't want you tripping on any horse apples and dropping our boy."

"I don't want to know what horse apples are, do I?" She handed over her son.

"You'll know. You'll be able to smell them long before you see them. Try not to step on one. You'll wreck those fancy athletic shoes you have on." As Sam settled Mikey in one arm, the baby stared up at him with big wide eyes.

"These are the most comfortable working shoes that I've ever owned." Grace glanced ahead on the path and eyed a suspicious lump of dirt. "Guess I should've bought boots before we left Fort Stockton."

Mikey reached up and patted Sam's cheek with the tips of his little fingers. Sam caught himself giving the kid a silly grin. Then he felt like the village idiot. These paternalistic impulses he was having were not appropriate and he needed to find a way of doing his job without all the emotion.

Clearing his throat, he said, "Careful as we enter the barn. They usually put down a combination of cement and boards for the aisles instead of using dirt like they use on the riding paths. And as I recall, the old boards were more uneven than the dirt. Easy to trip."

As they entered the cool shadowed recesses of the barn, and the smells of hay, manure and horseflesh assaulted his nose, Sam's shoulders relaxed. He had been gone too long.

At the first stall they came to, Mikey perked up. He pointed at the resident mare and squealed something in baby talk.

"Yes, Mikey," Grace said. "That's a horsey. Can you say horse?"

"Mum ma." Mikey bounced up and down on Sam's arm.

"No, baby. Horse."

"Rase!"

Sam chuckled. "Not quite. Maybe someday I'll take you for a ride. You'd like that."

As they continued ambling down the wide aisle past mainly closed stall doors, Grace looked over at Sam. "Do you ride well?"

"Used to. Haven't sat in the saddle since I left home to join the army."

Grace nodded thoughtfully. "It seems like you did all right here on the ranch with your family and the animals. It sounds like a perfect place for a kid. Did you always want to join the army? Is that why you left?"

"The military was an escape. That's all." Before she could question him further, he quickly went on to ask, "What did you want to study when you went to college?"

"I was a journalism major." She answered in a strong voice and without hesitation. "I wanted to be in newspapers like my dad."

"If you could do anything you want now, is that what you'd choose again?"

After taking a deep breath, she hedged, "I haven't given it a lot of thought."

Yeah, it figured that she wouldn't want to dwell on her past too much, either. He should've known that. Opening his mouth to say something—anything to get the two of them out of the mess they'd created for themselves, he was surprised when she spoke first.

"But I suppose if given my choice I would still want to write. Someday. Not so sure about newspapers, though. Maybe I'd like to try my hand at fiction instead."

They turned a corner and happened upon an open

stall holding a mare and a six-month-old colt. Mikey screeched and started bouncing and yelling.

"Raz! Raz!" He tried reaching out for the animals and squirmed, trying to get down.

Too late, Sam felt the baby slipping from the perch in the crick of his injured arm. Mikey headed in a nose dive toward the floor.

Both Sam and Grace jumped into action at the same time, grabbing for the child as he dropped. "Mikey!"

The next few moments lasted a lifetime. But when the dust settled, Sam found himself on his knees on the barn floor, holding Grace who was holding Mikey.

For a long time no one moved. Mikey seemed stunned into frozen silence. Grace was the first to breathe—and then she laughed.

"What's so funny?" Sam snapped.

"The look on your face is priceless." Grace's eyes sparked with amusement. "You're our hero. You saved us."

The way she was looking at him made his chest squeeze tight. But before he could come to his senses and mumble a reasonable remark back, Grace inched her face closer to his.

"We think that deserves a kiss as a reward. Right, Mikey?"

Sam stopped breathing as his eyes focused down on her lips. Those soft, kissable lips that were coming closer every second.

Grace told herself it was only a simple thank-you kiss. A playful, innocent thing to break the tension and pay him back for avoiding her questions.

So it made little sense that, from the moment her lips brushed his, she felt electric shivers running along her nerve endings. Sam was holding himself still—perfectly still with his eyes open. Who kissed someone with their eyes open?

But instead of breaking away as she normally would, Grace found herself closing her own eyes and breathing deeply through her nose. She smelled the lingering scent of his shaving cream and for some reason the smell drove her crazy. She'd noticed that same scent dozens of times before, but today it was one of the most sensual fragrances she could ever have imagined.

Without giving it enough thought, she used her tongue to nudge his lips, hoping he would deepen the kiss. For a few frozen moments she was sure he would be the one to break the kiss. But no. After a trembling hesitation, he increased the pressure of his mouth against hers and then parted his lips.

He tasted of coffee and crisp mornings—and home. And Grace's blood began to boil. What had she done?

His mouth was hot—as she'd known it would be. His hands were firm, strong yet gentle as he held both her and Mikey in his arms. She'd been fighting this attraction for months. She had no right to want an intimate relationship with this good man—or any other. No right at all.

But his kiss was perfect. Just right. And…

Fortunately for her, Mikey saved the day by beginning to squirm in his spot between them. The baby pounded his little fists against her chest and babbled his growing irritation about holding still for so long. Grace finally came to her senses and pulled back.

She struggled for a decent breath before saying, "It's…a little cold on the cement floor for Mikey. I think we'd better move."

"Right." Sam stood, pulling both her and Mikey up with him.

He glanced at her, checked her up and down, then released Mikey to her grasp.

Giving her a half smile, he both unnerved her and left her weak in the knees. She fought to rebuild the barriers they'd erected between them—sorry she'd broken the invisible and unwritten line that had been keeping them apart.

Scrambling to find something to divert attention from the tension darting between them, Grace set Mikey down on his feet, steadied him and held on to his tiny hands. "Let's walk, baby. Take a step for mama."

Any intimacy between her and Sam was out of the question. While staying on the ranch and learning more about how to survive, she needed him. At arm's length. But her two most important life missions were devoting full attention to raising her son, and learning how to stay out of the way of Jose Serrano and his pack of cutthroats.

As soon as he could gather his wits about him, Sam straightened up and said, "If you think the cement is too cold for Mikey, let's walk out the other side of the barn onto the dirt path. The sun has been warming the earth for most of the morning."

He was grateful to Mikey for becoming a distraction. For one crazy moment he'd thought about apologizing. But number one: she was the one who'd initiated the kiss. And number two: he wasn't the least bit sorry.

The only thing he was sorry for was that the kiss had ended too soon. He could've gone on kissing her for hours, days. Maybe for the rest of his life.

But that was such a disturbing notion, he decided it

was better to change the subject, concentrate on Mikey and get on with their walk.

Grace glanced over her shoulder at both ends of the barn, to where sunshine poured through open doors, and then nodded to him. "Good idea. He likes the horse barn just a little too much for a first outing."

As she looked up into Sam's face with a tentative smile, he felt the tension as strong as ever between them. And didn't care for it one bit. They were hiding out in a safe house, it didn't matter that the house happened to be his old home. The two of them must remain focused while in forced proximity for an undetermined amount of time. Lusting after each other would make the situation impossible.

Any continuation of this intense sexual attraction wouldn't do. He needed to find a way of making sure she never tried anything like that kiss again. The next time he might weaken entirely and be lost.

He understood that she saw him one way, and if nothing else, coming back here had convinced him he wasn't the kind of good guy she thought he was.

As they cleared the barn and headed out into the warm sunlight, he had a brilliant idea. She needed a healthy dose of reality where he was concerned.

"Grace, we need to talk."

With another quick glance in his direction, this one narrowed and wary, she telegraphed her opinion that the line might not have been the right way to start the conversation. But he had already dived into the water.

"I'm not who you think I am."

"What?" She picked up Mikey and clutched him to her breast. "What are you talking about?"

"I mean, I'm not really one of the good guys. I'll keep

you and Mikey safe from Serrano, but you need to keep yourself safe from me."

"You're not making any sense, Sam. I know you. And in the past couple of days you've proven your worth over and over."

He shook his head violently. "Listen to me. A long time ago I let my family down. Slithered off when they needed me the most. That's why I've stayed away for so long."

Glancing toward the distant river so he wouldn't have to watch her expression, Sam hurried on before he could lose his nerve. "If you get too close, I'll only let you down, too. Let me keep to myself and do my job."

"Excuse me? What a pile of horse apples! I don't buy any of that for one moment. You're the one who actually took a leave from your job to come find me and Mikey. If that's not being one of the good guys, I don't know what is."

She tenderly leaned her cheek against Mikey's hair and gazed at Sam with a longing look that took his breath. "And as far as letting you 'keep to yourself,' if you're talking about our kiss, both of us wanted that kiss and you know it. I won't force you to do anything you don't want to do—couldn't even if I tried. But Mikey and I need you nearby. There're things you can teach us. Things I want to know.

"So no good 'keeping to yourself,' pal," she went on. "You brought us here, now live with the consequences."

Dang, but the lady was sure something. He suddenly wanted her so badly he thought he might die of it. And that scared him much more than any lurking threat from a vengeful drug lord.

Chapter 9

Had she actually said those things? Dared to be that aggressive? Grace wondered what had come over her. Who had she suddenly become?

As they strolled back to the house in silence, she kept going over and over the bold moves she'd made, the daring things she'd said. Then she made herself stop all the self-doubting so she could consider her circumstances, her past and the man who was determined to save her.

Yes, once upon a time she'd been the kind of girl who would speak her mind and ask for what she wanted. She'd been proud and naive and full of herself. But Jose Serrano had taken all that away. For over five years now she'd been the mousy woman who stayed in his shadows, hoping not to be noticed and never smiling or speaking out.

The first big step away from Jose had come when

she'd learned she was pregnant with Mikey. The doctor offered an opportunity to break free and contact the FBI and she'd jumped at the chance. For her baby. For Mikey. Not for herself.

And when she'd spotted what she'd been sure were Serrano's men watching them in Denver, she'd taken off as fast and quietly as she possibly could. She'd left a man who had become a friend and all her government protection in the dust and didn't look back.

That sounded now like something a strong woman would do. But she hadn't felt strong. Only when Mikey was threatened did she become someone who could fight tigers.

Naturally her mind turned next to the kiss she and Sam had just shared. Something not even remotely due to Mikey. And the very idea that she would try anything like that surprised the devil out of her. She'd been teasing with Sam and had actually laughed. All the things she could scarcely remember doing in the past except with Mikey. Just think of that.

Who was she really?

As they came back inside Sam's childhood home and she took Mikey upstairs for a change, Grace saw in her mind's eye how much she, too, had been changing without her even noticing. She didn't know what to feel anymore. Nor who to be.

What she did know—that Sam was nearly as conflicted as she was—only made her more confused. But clearly he needed her to be strong. Almost as much as she needed the same from him. Was she strong enough to be everything?

When Mikey woke her up the next morning just at dawn, Grace dragged herself out of bed. She changed clothes and then took the baby to the bathroom for a quick cleanup. The whole while she felt restless. At odds within her own body.

The air seemed too close. Ready to smother her. But when she looked out the window, the weather looked perfect. The sun shone exactly the same as it had the day before.

She wondered if she was having premonitions about Jose finding them and that was why she felt so undefined and ill at ease.

Heading down the stairs with Mikey, she smelled coffee. It took her a moment to realize Sam must've gotten up before them. But in that moment she had a minor panic attack. Man, she hated feeling this helpless.

"Good morning." Sam turned his head to smile at her but went quickly back to work at the stove. "Hope you and Mikey like pancakes."

Sam was making breakfast? "I didn't know you could cook."

He didn't turn but she could hear the smile in his voice. "I wouldn't be much of a WITSEC officer unless I could keep both the witnesses and myself alive with basic cooking skills. And believe me, my skills are basic."

"How come you've never cooked for me?"

"You never needed me to cook. You did everything for yourself."

Had she? She vaguely remembered those first few months in hiding, wanting desperately to learn how to become completely self-sufficient. To be able to care for herself and her baby without help.

"I guess I was rebelling against Jose. He never let me lift a finger. Maybe he wanted to keep me on a pedestal like his mother. Or maybe he was afraid if I became too strong I would leave. Whatever it was, when I was finally free of him, I wanted to do everything on my own."

Sam nodded as he placed a stack of pancakes in front of her. "Syrup is warming on the stove. If you use butter, start there. Do you want me to give Mikey a pancake or simply a plate and let him share yours?"

She reminded him that Mikey had his own set of dishes. The ones made out of hard plastic that wouldn't break. Sam retrieved one from the dish drainer and put it on the high chair's tray table. Then he handed her the syrup. She hurriedly cut up one dry pancake for the baby and put it in his dish.

Mikey seemed pleased—and hungry—and dug in with his fingers. Good thing her son didn't like syrup or butter yet.

Grace wished she was as hungry as he was. She'd lost her appetite somewhere last night. But the pancakes did look good.

She sat there staring at them, lost in thought, just a little too long.

"I didn't poison yours, I promise." Sam sat down on the opposite side of the table. "Mikey seems to like his and I'll take a bite of my own if it'll make you feel any better. You're going to need your strength. Travis called a little while ago. Seems Jenna won't eat or sleep unless she gets to see the baby today."

"No problem about Jenna and I'm sure the pancakes are great. It's just…" She looked over at Sam and his eyes narrowed. Nearly laughing aloud, she wanted to tell him that he needn't worry. She didn't feel like either kissing or talking this morning.

"Sam, I need you to do something for me."

After a long moment's hesitation, during which he

downed a short stack, he cleared his throat and said, "What would that be?"

"Teach me how to shoot a gun. I saw a glass case in the other room that's full of rifles—or maybe they're shotguns. Anyway, teach me how to fire one, please."

Sam dropped his fork on his plate with a clatter. "That's not a good idea. If you're worried about Serrano, let me handle it. That's my job."

"No, it's not. You're on leave. And besides, a whole gang of Jose's men may show up at any moment. I want to be able to help."

"Guns shouldn't be used by amateurs. If you came face-to-face with Serrano's men and one of them was a man you happened to know from your time there, could you shoot him?"

Good question. But then she thought of Mikey. "Yes. If my baby was on the line, I wouldn't hesitate to pull the trigger."

Sam smiled. "Okay, mama bear, I believe you. But guns are still a bad idea. What if someone overpowers you and turns the weapon on you and Mikey?"

"I wouldn't have the gun in my hand in the first place if I didn't have every intention of using it."

That wiped the smile from his face. "Good answer. But not one I'm sure I really believe."

After taking a big gulp from his coffee mug, he continued, "Okay. You probably need something to occupy your mind while we're on the ranch anyway. But if I agree to this, you will have to do it my way."

"What does that mean? What's your way?"

The smile on his face now seemed like a wry grin— and not a particularly friendly one. "You will learn as I learned from my father. The same way army recruits are trained. First you will learn the parts of a weapon.

Next you will learn to tear one down, clean it and put it back together again. Before you ever load one or point it at a target, the weapon will become your most intimate friend."

"Is that really necessary?"

"It is if you want me to be your teacher."

All of his demands seemed totally unnecessary. As if he thought making her go through innumerable tedious steps would make her give up the whole idea.

Well, he was wrong about that. "Fine. Can we start today?"

While Grace did the breakfast dishes and Mikey played on the floor with a few pots and spoons, Sam went upstairs to the original wing and his father's library. The old door stuck and he had to use shoulder power to force it open. When he stepped inside the seldom-used room, both memories and dust motes assaulted his senses.

He'd come here to find his father's rifle manuals. The ones he had so hated reading as a boy. He hoped to hell they would discourage Grace as much as they had almost discouraged him as a child.

It had been a full five years after his father's death before Sam could admit to himself that the old man had been right to insist on his learning the basics before taking a gun in hand. But at eight years old all he could think was how deprived he felt in having to *read* when all his school buddies were already practicing with BB guns and targets.

Sitting in his father's worn-out easy chair, Sam looked around the familiar room. Like something out of a half-remembered dream, images surrounded him. On the top shelf in the left-hand corner he spied the family Bible and photo albums. He could almost say from memory what pictures were pasted in those albums and on what pages. It might be interesting to see if his memory was still good, but Sam wasn't sure he felt steady enough to go through them yet.

In the distance he heard a vehicle pulling up in front of the house. Must be his brother and Jenna. Thinking about summer, his eyes landed on the top right-hand shelf, where his mother's collection of cookbooks had been stored. Just the sight of them and the images of her using one or the other in the kitchen while she prepared a birthday or anniversary meal gave him an ache that felt exactly like someone had put a bullet dead center of his chest. No, he wouldn't be touching those books anytime soon.

The middle rows were filled, as they always had been, with his father's collection of fiction, peppered liberally with his favorite biographies. Louis L'Amour Westerns. A few legal and military thrillers and a handful of old classics. His father had eclectic tastes. Sam remembered borrowing many of them on long winters' nights.

He let his gaze drift down to the bottom rows of technical manuals. *Range Management. A Guide to Raising Chickens.* Sam flashed back to his father helping him with a 4-H project. That particular manual had been invaluable at settling arguments.

Next he noted the rifle manuals that were right where he'd put them the last time he'd had to open them almost thirty years ago. He reached for the first book but his hand nearly landed on a set of psychological texts instead. Sitting back, he tried to think back to what those university books were doing on his father's shelves.

He did vaguely remember the texts from his youth,

he'd even read one or two. Oh, yeah, now he recalled that his mother had been going to college as a psychology major when she'd met his dad.

Sam had once been most interested in the sections on criminal behavior. Back when he'd wanted to be a lawman when he grew up. Back before his father insisted he would do no such thing.

Automatically Sam's mind made the connection from criminal behavior to Jose Serrano, and he couldn't help wondering what the drug lord was up to. As Sam saw him, Serrano was a typical Latin male, wound up tight with his machismo heritage. It would only be a matter of time before Jose lost control and went on a rampage to find his son.

Sam heard female footsteps coming down the hall but the door opened before he could rise.

"Sammy! Darlin'. Jenna insisted we stop in to see you. Come give your auntie a hug, son. It's been such a long time."

Sam stood, turned and found himself staring into the face of a woman whose features so resembled his father's that a sudden melancholy threatened to choke him. "Auntie June."

He stood and kissed her cheek. "It's good to see you. Don't tell me Jenna talked you into bringing her out here. I'm not so sure that's a good idea."

"No? Why ever not? All that girl will talk about is the adorable new baby on the ranch. Besides, I wanted to see one of my favorite nephews again."

He started to tell her he was using the place as a safe house, and it might not be wise to advertise the fact that a baby was in residence. But then he realized that was nonsense. People would know he had brought a child onto the ranch. Chance was too small to keep it a secret for long.

But just as sure as he was that the people of Chance would know Mikey was there, he also knew Serrano would come eventually. And it was Sam's duty to be prepared for him.

Chapter 10

The sleek black Hummer with armor-plated sides sped across the Chihuahuan Desert, taking Jose Serrano to Ciudad Juárez and the headquarters of one of his lieutenants.

Jose's U.S. Marshals Service contact had come up with a couple of possible places in the United States. Spots where the lawman who'd been hiding Jose's son might have his own contacts and would feel protected.

Both places were in the southwestern section of the United States and Jose was confident that either would be easy for his men to penetrate. Sure it would only be a matter of days, or at most a week or two, he relaxed, thinking his son would soon be safely under his control and at home with Jose's mother.

Sitting comfortably in the luxurious backseat as his driver and bodyguard kept careful watch out the windshield, Jose stretched out and took a moment to consider his next steps. The more he thought about that American woman's treachery and her U.S. lawman's duplicity, the more Jose became convinced that both of them deserved to die. But carefully. With finesse. And only after Jose's son was out of their control and removed from the line of fire.

His satellite phone rang, interrupting Jose's thoughts. He answered, only to find disturbing news from a henchman on the other end.

"It is true, jefe. We have cleared the Phoenix area. That is where the gringo lived when he first worked for the Marshals' Service and took college courses. His neighbors there claim not to have heard from him in years. None of his army amigos have been in contact with him in over a decade, either. At least they won't admit to it."

Jose felt the slow burn of temper creeping up his throat. But this was only a setback, not the end game.

"Move on, then," he told his man through gritted teeth. "What is the next place on your list?"

"A small town in Texas. Where the gringo grew up. But when we phoned the sheriff's office, we were told our target left the place nearly fifteen years ago and had never returned. Not even for the funeral of his father."

Jose thought about his feelings toward family. When *he* needed a safe place, he went home. He trusted no one as much as he trusted his cousins.

"Do not expect the *Americanos* to tell you the truth." During his years spent in California, he'd discovered Anglos had no fear of lying in order to get their way or to save their asses. "You must go there. See for yourself. But be careful. You do not want to arouse suspicions or the gringo will run."

"I have a plan for learning truth in this small town,

jefe." Hector sounded smug and Jose listened with interest. "Pedro and I will ask for temporary work. We will use the fake identification you provided. Once we are working, the *Americanos* will have no fear of talking to us."

It wasn't a half-bad plan. Jose could have thought of it himself if he'd had the time. For a second he worried that this clever employee might prove to be too smart— in a devious way.

The first rule Jose had ever learned for staying in power was to watch his back. As the Anglos said, "Keep your friends close and your enemies closer." It seemed particularly true in Mexico these days.

Jose thought all of those things, but what he said was, "An excellent plan. I will stay nearby—just across the border. Keep me informed."

Hanging up, Jose eased out a breath and nodded to himself. Yes, an excellent plan. But the child was his— his son. And he intended to stay extremely close.

He tapped on the glass between front and back seats and captured the attention of his driver and bodyguard.

When the glass was opened he said, "I wish to cross into the United States at the Texas border. Change course and head for our compound at Ciudad Acuña."

The bodyguard blinked and his lips tightened. "But, jefe, you are a wanted man in the United States of America and the border has become *muy* dangerous. Perhaps…"

"It's your job to keep me away from the authorities and out of the line of fire." Jose did not need this imbecile telling him about danger. "Do your job or I will find someone who can."

Most of the danger on the Texas border came from his own men and their increasing drug and weapons smuggling in the rural areas. Finding a way across the border there would be easier than trying it in a more populated and patrolled city.

Jose thought again of the prize for taking this much risk. His son. He had never been allowed to see his own son. The thought of such injustice set his teeth on edge.

The only reason he knew about the baby was from those first few days in court in Los Angeles. Grace. His beautiful little Bella now made over into Grace—the traitor—had been there to testify against him. And it had been abundantly clear that she was with child. His child. The timing told the story.

After that Jose had been more ardent in his attempts to escape. He'd had to pay a king's ransom to his contact in the U.S. in order to escape during an emergency dental trip. But he had been determined. And everyone knew you could not stop Jose Serrano once his mind was decided.

Just as he had now decided to enter the U.S. again to pick up his son and bring him home.

Nothing. No one. Would stand in his way.

Chapter 11

It turned out Grace was good with guns. At least she'd had little trouble with the Remington Model 870 Express pump action shotgun that Sam insisted she use for practice.

For two straight days she'd read every manual in his collection. Next she broke down the shotgun into its subparts, cleaned it and put it all back together. By now she knew every minute detail: the three-inch chamber, the twenty-one-inch vent rib barrel, the choke, the pull and every gleaming inch of the hardwood stock. The shotgun had been Sam's as a boy. And as she'd stroked and polished the wood she thought of him—and began to hunger.

This afternoon while his aunt June was watching Mikey and Jenna over at Travis's house, Grace and Sam were on their way to practice shooting down by the river behind the house. For their entire tramp through the fields she'd been arguing with herself and trying not to notice the scent of his shaving cream or the way his jeans rode on his hips.

A few days of working together and living in the same house, and Sam had not made one move to repeat the kiss of the other day.

Grace had been so engrossed with her learning, and watching as Sam read and played with the baby, that she hadn't given much thought to why she needed all this information and practice in the first place.

But as the sun began to wane in the sky and the two of them walked closer to the river where no cattle were being kept over the winter, she felt depressed. The more she learned, the better able she was to care for herself and her son, and the sooner she could take off and let Sam escape back into his real world. His real job.

The man had saved her son and offered her safety. Little by little she'd begun making a subconscious place for him in her heart. But she couldn't allow that to continue. Yes, she longed to really know how the two of them would be together, both intimately and over the long haul. He was a superb specimen of a man. Tall and lanky, hard and tender. What woman wouldn't want to know that strength and gentleness for a lifetime?

But she didn't deserve such a prize. She'd given away her virtue—her very soul—to a bastard who had no merit. Jose Serrano wasn't worthy of licking the boots of a man like Sam Chance.

Yes, sometimes it was tough to keep from either flirting with him or begging for him to kiss her. But it was clear Sam wouldn't want to be saddled with a woman and a child. His life was on the move for the Marshals, away from family and home. Over the past day or so she'd become increasingly aware that the man was itch-ing to leave Chance and go back to his job. Something about his old home and his family was causing Sam to want to run—just like she had done.

Whereas now, she was starting to feel a little too comfortable. Sam's brother, Jenna and June were all so open and loving with her and Mikey. She could easily imagine making a place for her and her son here. But there was no way. Eventually Jose would find them. And when he did, it would not be pretty for those nearby.

She had to stay on the move. It was the only way to keep Mikey safe and at the same time protect those people who had taken them in and had been so kind.

She'd already been the cause of one huge screwup in her lifetime. A screwup so horrific she couldn't bear to think about it. People she'd loved had died. And she didn't deserve a second chance.

But none of it had ever been Mikey's fault. Or Sam's.

"You're being particularly quiet," Sam said as he slowed his pace to walk beside her. "Are you going over in your head the parts of the gun and the sequence for taking a shot?" He spoke for the first time in ten minutes and she was particularly glad to hear his voice.

Earlier today he'd set up a target down by the river. Now she carried the shotgun, in the prescribed method for walking, and he carried the box of shells.

"No, not really. I'm not worried about the target practice. I've been concentrating on the reason for the lesson."

"Serrano? Don't…"

Shaking her head, she smiled. "No, not Jose. Mikey."

"He's okay with June and Jenna."

"Oh, I know that. He's thriving. I've never seen him so happy for such a prolonged period. He really seems to love the ranch."

"He knows he's safe here." Sam put his hand on her shoulder. "Children pick up on the vibes of their parents. He can tell when you are anxious or afraid. You've been more relaxed over the past few days."

"Have I?" The warmth of his hand went right through her thin jacket and straight to her belly. She suddenly didn't feel one bit relaxed.

Even Sam seemed to notice the spark between them. He removed his hand and stared at it for a second—as though he'd gotten a static shock.

Rubbing his palm over his jeans, he picked up the pace and took off toward the target. "Let's get a move on before we lose the light."

Something was going on inside that beautiful head, Sam decided. Something besides the lust. He'd seen the look of longing apparent on Grace's face again today, and felt that accidental touch of hands. He was experiencing the exact same thing. It had been all he could do to keep from making an overt move toward her that might lead Grace to believe they had any chance of acting on their instincts.

He let out a deep breath. So, the lust was a given. Grinding his teeth, he kept walking. But something else was also happening inside her mind. He'd seen an unusual look in her eyes now and then. A sadness. An expression of defeat.

Over the past couple of days as she'd been reading his father's gun manuals, he'd stayed close. But he'd been studying his mother's old psychology texts. He was looking for something useful to help Grace.

He'd come to the conclusion that she was suffering from PTSD and she'd probably also had a bad case of Stockholm syndrome while being held by Serrano.

While he was no psychiatrist, all the symptoms and causes seemed clear enough.

She needed professional help, and he wondered if he dared to broach the subject with her. He cared about Grace and Mikey. More than he had any right to. And while he couldn't think in terms of forever with them, he wanted to do everything in his power to help.

The books had said Stockholm syndrome sufferers needed love and support from family. But all Grace seemed to have was Mikey.

They reached the spot where he'd set up the target and he paced off thirty feet. "Okay. This is the distance. Any closer and the bad guys could overpower you. Any farther and you won't have as good a chance of hitting your target."

"It would be hard to miss from here."

He chuckled at her bravado. "Have you ever shot any kind of weapon before?"

"Never."

"Well, then, let's see how you do before you get too cocky."

She raised the shotgun and held out her hand. "Twenty-gauge, please."

Opening the box, he cautioned, "You remember your lesson on loading? It can be a little tricky."

She gave him a look that could've frozen a tropical ocean. "I remember."

Going through all the right moves to load and pump the shotgun, she seemed smooth and professional. Sam was vacillating between proud and worried.

"Don't forget about the noise. And the kick."

He couldn't stand the thought of the Remington either biting into her shoulder or putting her on her butt. This target practice had been a terrible idea.

"Maybe we should've started with a BB gun," he offered.

Grace gave him another icy look, but then her eyes softened. "Can you show me the best way to hold the gun in order to fire? Now that we're out here, everything feels different."

That was bull. She was perfectly capable of firing a ladies-size shotgun without a second's thought, and he knew it. But it would make him feel a little better if he stood behind her to shield her from any potential kick.

Just until she got the hang of it, mind you.

He moved in close to her back and put his hands on her shoulders. "All right. Like we practiced inside. Plant your feet."

She did as he asked and he braced her legs with his own. They were close enough now that he could feel her heat, rising up through her coat and jeans. He smelled her shampoo, and the scent nearly made him light-headed.

"Er... Okay. Now raise the shotgun and sight the target. Prepare to fire."

"That'll be easy," she whispered. "I'm pretending it's Jose's face on that target. I won't miss."

Her words stopped him for a second. Was that typical of Stockholm syndrome victims? To want to kill their captors? Vengeance was never a good reason to fire a gun.

It was too late to stop their lesson so Sam ran his hands down her arms to show her the proper hold on the shotgun. She was just the right size for him to reach around and help. Truthfully she was just about the right everything. He was getting hard standing this close and touching her, and it was all he could do to concentrate on the weapon in her arms. Man, this lesson had to be over soon.

"Now, place your finger on the trigger." His voice was hoarse, his eyes blurring. "Nice and easy does it."

"Uh…Sam?" She suddenly sounded so tentative that he nearly ripped the danged gun out of her hands.

"What's wrong?"

"You're standing too close. I can hardly breathe."

"Just pull the frigging trigger."

The shot came slow and easy. Just like they'd practiced. And the kick was a lightweight, hardly worth mentioning. He felt like an idiot for worrying.

Stepping back, he cleared his throat. "Nice work. You hit the target dead-on. You're a natural shot."

"Like I said, all I have to do is visualize Jose. Can I practice some more?"

"Uh, sure. Go ahead."

He let her go through the entire process alone the next time. And the next. Load. Aim. Fire.

She was a deadeye with the target. But if she was faced with the reality of a man instead of a target, would she freeze?

He remembered the first time he'd ever fired on a real man, the enemy, in the service. It had been all he could do to pull the trigger. In his very first platoon there had been many a young kid who couldn't fire their weapon when it came right down to a firefight with the enemy. A few of those same fine American youths were now lying in their graves.

When Sam had moved on to the MPs, the idea of firing on one of his own soldiers had turned his stomach. In reality he'd never had to actually do it. A couple of good raps on the head and a few nights spent in the stockade had been all it took to straighten out soldiers who were acting out being scared and missing home.

Looking over at Grace, he wondered what he could possibly do to help her straighten out. She was scared and didn't have a home to go to. A situation not much different from new recruits.

She fired again. And once again she hit the target dead center. Well, at least she was a much better shot than most young army recruits.

"You had enough yet? You've massacred Serrano at least a dozen times."

"I don't feel ready." She turned to speak and Sam could see the determination mixed liberally with fear on her face.

This whole idea had not been very bright. He was sorry now he'd ever agreed to it.

"What if whoever comes after me is running toward me? How can I be sure I can hit a moving target?"

"They probably *will* be running toward you. If they're running away, save the shells."

"Not funny, Sam. I mean it. I'm more scared now than I was before we started."

"Scared is good. It means you'll be careful."

Her shoulders slumped. "I'm tired of being scared. I can't keep running my whole life. I want to be able to take a stand."

From a strictly psychological standpoint, her attitude was probably good. From the standpoint of facing a drug lord and his gang, however, her attitude would probably get her killed.

And Grace dead was not a concept he could accept. Not now. Not ever.

How could he help her? Maybe she needed more

practice. Or maybe a semiautomatic handgun where she could shoot at a moving target multiple times.

"I'm done." Her voice was so low he could barely hear her words. "Let's go to the house."

He helped her police the area and they started back. Yeah, maybe what she needed was a different weapon. But she also needed something else. Some nebulous something he was at a loss to provide. She seemed so down and that was not like the Grace he'd come to admire.

As they tramped over the fields, she kept slipping and sliding due to her work shoes. He took charge of the shotgun and grabbed her elbow to help her walk upright.

"Thanks," she mumbled. "I'm such a disaster. I don't know why you even bother with me."

"You're no such thing. All you need is a good pair of boots. That's an easy fix."

Just as they were about to enter the yard surrounding his old home, Grace managed to traipse through a cow cake. Ancient as it was, the sticky bits still did a number on her shoes.

"Look at this mess." She looked about ready to cry. "I'm a total screwup."

"No you're not." But Sam knew his words weren't going to make much of an impression on her in this state.

He needed an idea for a jolt that would shake her out of the mood. She was a beautiful, talented woman who made one of the best mothers he'd ever met. Yet somehow she didn't have a clue.

A nightstick over the head wasn't going to make the kind of impression he wanted this time. Not like with the young recruits. So what…?

They'd reached the house. "Why don't you sit on the

porch step and kick off your shoes. We can rinse them off later."

She did as he suggested. Meanwhile he stashed the unloaded shotgun right inside the back door. She could clean and store that later, too.

Standing, Grace hobbled toward the door in her stocking feet. "Don't watch me. I must look like an invalid."

He reached down and swung her up in his arms. "Quiet. You're a beautiful woman. And I intend to prove it to you—right now."

Chapter 12

Grace nearly swallowed her tongue as Sam hoisted her in his arms and kicked the door open. "Wait. I can walk."

"Quiet. I'll do the walking. And the talking."

She bit her lip and waited for him to deposit her on the family room sofa. But he didn't stop. He hefted her against his broad chest and practically raced up the stairs. Then without even breathing heavy, he barged right into the master bedroom she'd been using and swung her around like she was a lightweight.

She was no lightweight. Hadn't been since Mikey was born.

Gently, he bent to lay her on the huge bed. The minute he straightened, she started to scramble off.

His wide palm came down on her stomach. "Stay put."

He reached for her socks, pulled them free in two

quick moves. Then he reached for her waistband, undid the button and zipper and had her jeans in a pile on the floor before she could blink.

"Uh…"

"Shush." He took one of her legs between his big hands and began languidly stoking the flesh on her calf. "These legs don't look like they belong to an *invalid* to me. They're sexy as hell."

"Uh…" Lying before him in nothing but her T-shirt and panties was making her hot. And the gleam in his eyes wasn't helping to cool things down.

Sam let go of her leg and reached up to grab the edge of her T-shirt, pulling it over her head in one swift move. She shifted to help him peel it off, then lay back down and looked up at him through eyelids blurred by the intense heat he'd stirred.

He sat beside her on the bed and began messaging one arm. Wrist to shoulder. "And this arm is definitely not a *disaster.*"

After a few minutes of tantalizing her nearly beyond endurance, he helped her to sit up. But he quickly slid in behind her and wouldn't let her turn to see his face. If Jose had made such a move, she would've been frightened by what was coming next. But this wasn't Jose. Not even close.

Sam began massaging her shoulders. "Tight. But I'm not feeling any *screwup* under my hands. In fact, I can't find any part of you that is anything but beautiful and strong."

She moaned and tried to turn again but he held her steady.

"You're a sexy, powerful woman, Grace," he whispered.

His fingers slipped down her back. So slowly she

felt like screaming. She sure hoped she knew what was coming. And coming soon.

Suddenly her bra was undone, sliding across her body and joining her jeans on the floor. Now she was almost naked and he still had on all his clothes.

Grace had no idea how to ask for what she wanted. What she needed. She'd forgotten how. Or maybe it was more like she had never known how.

Now she was left feeling like a foolish virgin without a clue what to do or say. Pretty funny, really. A virgin with a nearly one-year-old son.

Her shoulders sagged at the half-baked joke. The joke on her. A decent man like Sam deserved someone who was whole and could make him happy—in every way.

The hand that had been slipping down her back gently gripped her shoulder. From behind her she heard his boots hitting the carpet—one after the other. Then the whooshing of material as he must've removed his clothes. The next thing she knew, he was surrounding her with his long legs, still encased in jeans. After he snuggled up close behind her, she felt his naked, hairy chest against her back. So he'd removed his shirt. But why not everything?

Before she had a chance to become too curious, his hands came around her rib cage, his fingers lingering on her breasts. With just the barest of touches, her whole body jerked in response.

"Easy does it." He stopped moving his fingers, resting his palms against her nipples and letting their gentle warmth seep into her skin. He waited, until finally she thought she might burn up with the fever.

"Sam, hurry. I…"

"I won't hurt you, Grace. Patience. This is for you and it's better slow."

Sam surprised her. Jose had never touched her that way, and had never bothered to speak to her at all. He'd always been in a hurry. Ripping and pawing at her until he got what he wanted.

Sam's hands began lightly stroking her nipples as if her breasts were made of the softest silk. She soon lost herself in the sensations consuming her, feeling hot and sexy yet safe at the same time.

She wanted to touch Sam in return, to somehow give him the same sort of wonderful erotic massage. But he wouldn't let her turn. All right, if this was how he insisted it go, for now she would try to relax and enjoy. Grabbing on to his thighs with a vicelike grip, she leaned back against his chest and closed her eyes.

"Relax, beautiful," he whispered close to her ear. "You're too tense. Let yourself go loose. You deserve a little pleasure."

Suddenly it occurred to her that it had been a long time since a man had seen her naked. And that man had barely stopped long enough to look. From Sam's vantage point, he could see everything.

But she wasn't the least embarrassed or nervous with Sam and wanted him to keep going. So she let loose of his jeans and flexed her hands, trying not to fist them again.

His fingers glided down her chest, circled her belly button and slipped under the waistband of her very plain panties. Now she felt embarrassed that she hadn't thought to buy at least one pair of sexy underwear. She bit her lip, closed her eyes and fought to stay loose.

Don't stop now.

This slow torture was…was… Pure pleasure.

At a loss for words, she held her breath. Sam's fingers tangled in the curls at the apex of her thighs and her legs fell open—all by themselves. Really.

Would he think her too wanton? Too needy? At this point it didn't much matter what he thought. Just as long as he kept going.

With the gentlest of touches, one of his hands cupped her breast while the other stroked the tender place between her legs. She wouldn't mind if he speeded things up—just a little. But he kept stroking. Slowly. Softly. Patiently. His fingers touched her, over and over, adding electricity and warmth with every pass. The ache inside her turned to desperation.

Squirming, her hips lifted off the bed. She felt the tension curling up to capture her entire body. How was she supposed to sit still through this?

She gave herself permission to moan. He couldn't mind that, could he? But as pitiful little sounds began to emerge from her throat, she realized this whole experience was unique. Sam actually seemed to like hearing her sounds of pleasure.

He began murmuring encouragement and hushed words of endearment, but she could barely focus on anything, save for the feelings building inside her.

Sliding one finger inside her warm depths, Sam began teasing her with his moves, in and out, pushing her toward some higher plane. But it still didn't seem like enough. She wanted him to feel these wondrous sensations right along with her.

Frustrated, she was helpless to beg for more. Helpless to do anything but rock her hips and listen to her own moans growing louder and louder.

"Please, Sam…"

His touches remained steady, tender, until she thought she might actually go crazy. The aching in her groin and the electricity running up and down her limbs built toward something just out of reach. Something totally unexpected but desperately sought.

Her every feeling now seemed brand-new and magnified tenfold. She was growing more and more edgy, reaching out for some elusive gate to the unknown.

Then without warning, Grace exploded. A blast that rocketed her off center. Stars burst behind her eyelids, and it was all she could do to hold it together and concentrate on the most amazing feelings ever.

When she came back down to reality, Sam was cradling her in his arms. He swept light kisses across her face and mouth, making her feel wanted and safe enough to continue lying still. Luxuriating in the feelings as the static pulses continued bouncing inside, she sighed aloud.

But she'd expected more ardent moves from him. More insistent. He didn't appear to be in any rush.

In another moment she realized his kisses were much too tame, not passionate in the least. "Sam? Don't you want…?"

"Another time. It was my pleasure to show you that you are indeed a beautiful woman—in every way."

"I never knew it could be so wonderful."

"I guessed."

She lifted her head to look in his eyes. "Thank you."

"No," he said softly. "Thank *you*. I haven't been in the presence of such peace and beauty in a very long time."

Sam was so unlike Jose it stunned her for the moment. He was unselfish And generous to a fault.

All of a sudden she felt greedy and selfish. And she

didn't like the feeling at all. "But…seriously, Sam. When do *you* get a turn?"

"Nothing says I have to. I'm good."

"I'll say you are. But…" Had she changed enough over the past few weeks to ask for—no—to *demand* what she wanted?

"What if I wanted another turn? This time my treat." Well, guess *that* demand answered her question. She held her breath and waited for an answer.

A smile broke the serious look on his face. "I don't believe I've ever had a more compelling offer. Sounds good to me."

"Really? When?" She rose up on her elbow and tried to ignore the fact that she was still half-naked.

The same sad, remote look she'd noticed over the past days filled his eyes for a moment. But then he blinked it away. And this time when his gaze landed on her, the look he gave her was so erotic it ignited a bonfire at her core.

"There's something we need to take care of first."

"What?" She hoped against hope he wasn't about to say they had to get rid of Jose Serrano before anything else happened. That jerk had ruled her every move for far too long.

"We need to make a trip to town," he said with a wry grin. "I think it's time you got yourself a decent pair of boots. And I need to stop in to visit my brother Gage. Travis tells me he's been back in town from a business trip for a few days, but I haven't heard a word from him."

Those didn't seem like good enough reasons for why they couldn't continue what they'd started right now. Not in her opinion. "When are we going?"

"Tomorrow morning."

"But that means we have until Mikey comes back here tonight. Why couldn't we…?"

"In the first place, we have one more stop to make tomorrow. I wouldn't be much of a bodyguard if I didn't make sure we had protection. This—" he waved a hand between them "—came as a…surprise and I wasn't prepared."

"Oh." He wanted to protect them?

He must know she'd been checked over by every specialist the FBI had when she'd first escaped Jose and was declared physically fit—if not mentally stable. And as her guardian, he was well aware of her currently self-imposed celibate state.

So he was truly concerned about *her* welfare. How about that? The man was too good.

Probably too good for her in the long haul. But Grace wasn't thinking of the long haul at the moment. In a few days or a couple of weeks, she planned to disappear again anyway. But before she went, she intended to find that magic edge with Sam at least once more.

And that time, he would be going over the edge along with her. She'd never felt so sure of anything in her whole life.

Outside on the porch Sam took a couple of deep breaths. He'd had to leave Grace to take her shower alone before he weakened and joined her.

Staring down at her filthy shoes, he decided that removing crap would make a perfect occupation for a man who'd apparently lost his mind. He picked the shoes up by their laces and walked around the house to the hose.

While pouring water over them, he stretched his shoulders and stared up at the sky. The first of the evening stars were already visible and a half-moon had made its early appearance on the horizon.

His mind went back to a few moments ago with Grace. The trust she had given him was astounding. It had touched him in a way nothing had for as long as he could remember. Oh, sure, before tonight, she'd trusted him to be a good protector. But that was only his job. This time she'd turned over her body to his care.

Despite his multiple misgivings about his own steadfastness, he refused to let her down. He would not disappear from her life the way he'd done to his own family years ago.

Maybe he could change. Maybe he'd already started to change.

Putting away the hose and carting the soaked shoes back to the porch to dry, Sam decided to take the time to clean the shotgun, too. Tomorrow would be soon enough for her to learn that particular lesson. And tonight he thought she needed a break.

He sat on his mother's rocking chair and worked at cleaning his childhood gun. Darkness engulfed him under the shelter of the porch roof, but he didn't need light to find every inch of the weapon. He could've cleaned the old Remington in his sleep.

Familiar nighttime noises: the rustling of crisp breezes through the cottonwoods around the house; the first of the katydids getting ready for their spring mating; the soft snuffling of horses in the corrals, took his imagination back to his boyhood and the many nights he'd spent out on the plain with his father's ranch hands. The only things missing tonight were the sounds of cattle softly stirring through the darkness. But in his mind he could hear them still.

As he worked and listened, the soft, familiar sounds

of evening changed their tone. The winds suddenly seemed ominous. Peering into the distance, Sam stared through the deep night shadows and thought he saw movement. Every leaf, every blade of grass appeared like a specter in his mind.

It wasn't possible that Serrano's men could've found them so quickly. And even if they somehow guessed he'd brought Mikey and Grace to Chance, they would play hell getting on the ranch without being stopped. Too many gates and too many ranch hands who knew better than to allow strangers on the land.

Yet as impossible as he believed it was, his gut told him Serrano was getting close. Tomorrow morning Sam would have to make a few attempts at disguise so they could go into town undetected by any strangers.

A few other ideas for misdirection came into his mind, too. Along with his earlier idea for obtaining another gun for Grace. A little more security around the house might be in order, as well.

The hair on his arms stood on end as even the insects went silent. Perhaps her idea of confronting the monster by being prepared would be for the best. Meet the enemy straight out and get it over with.

Because whatever else Sam did or did not do to prepare, he felt another confrontation was coming. And coming soon.

Chapter 13

Hector Robles drove a pickup along a ranch-to-market road near Chance, Texas, in the early spring sunshine. Hector's partner, Pedro, sat shotgun. The truck belonged to Chance County rancher big Jim Ed Thacker.

The men were performing duties for their new jobs, running errands for Thacker's Double-T ranch. Being ranch gophers didn't pay much, but then the work gave them both plenty of reason to meet the people of Chance and hear local gossip.

Almost to Main Street, Hector downshifted and said, "I think we need different jobs. Something that gets us closer to the interior of the Chance ranch."

"Then you believe that rumor of a baby living at the old Chance homestead is true? You haven't informed Senor Serrano."

Hector didn't bother answering. Sometimes he got sick and tired of explaining things to Pedro.

"How do you plan on getting close to the old homestead?" Pedro leaned forward in his seat until the seat belt cut into his thick neck. "That casa is supposed to be miles inside the last gates. And word is, the background of everybody who gets hired out there is checked and double-checked. Seems to me, they act like they're expecting trouble."

"Of course they are. That's what makes me so sure the rumors are true."

But Hector was ten moves ahead of whoever made the rules for the Bar-C. He had it all figured out. Now he simply had to put his plan into action.

"Admit it," Pedro whined. "They're too smart for us. And Serrano will kill us if we can't capture his baby alive."

There were times when Hector would be grateful to Serrano for putting a bullet hole between Pedro's eyes. First, however, he needed his partner's added gunpower.

To have any hope of even getting that far, Hector needed to find a way of keeping his damned partner's big mouth shut. "Don't talk anymore. Don't say a word. Especially around strangers. Let me do all the talking— and all the thinking."

Pedro shut up, but his stare was sending threats.

Okay, Hector wouldn't mind killing his idiot partner even if Serrano didn't do it for him.

Right after they safely tucked the baby into the boss's waiting arms. Hector figured it wouldn't be long now.

As they made their last stop at the Feed and Seed Store, Hector got the news he'd been waiting to hear from one of the stockboys. A contractor was in town hiring temporary hands for spring cutting on the Bar-C.

Spring on a huge place like the Bar-C, where they

raised sheep and angora goats in addition to quarter horses and cattle, was the busiest time of year. Sheep and goats needed to be sheared. Cows needed cutting and weaning, castrating and branding. Horses would have to be broke, castrated and earmarked.

There'd be plenty of work for fifty or more good men in addition to the regular ranch employees. And as dull as Pedro was, he was good with a rope and a horse. Hector, too, had been raised on an estancia before he'd migrated to Los Angeles and joined Serrano's gang. He could handle any job on the ranch that they chose to give him.

Ranch work was hard but it would give them the opportunity to learn the lay of the land and look for an opening to reach the baby.

"Are we going to the diner to apply for jobs?"

Hector could hear his partner's stomach growling from here but the diner was clear on the other side of town. "Yes. But we apply for work first—then eat. Keep your mind on the prize. Believe me, the *patron* will know if you don't."

"But Serrano is in Mexico."

"Don't count on that being true. Serrano is a smart man who has lots of friends in the U.S. I wouldn't put it past him to be in hiding here in Texas. And watching us."

Pedro actually turned his head to check through all the pickup's windows, looking for any sign of the boss.

Hector didn't for one minute believe Serrano could get over the border with every lawman in America looking for him. But he wouldn't put it past the smart drug lord to hire more people to follow them around, waiting for any slipup. He and Pedro needed to be alert.

Hector had to park down the block from the diner.

Apparently many men had heard about the contractor. He would have to be smarter and stronger to get hired.

As he jumped from the pickup's cab and his boots hit the asphalt street, Hector couldn't help but checking around himself—just to see if anyone was watching.

He didn't notice anyone or anything out of place. But as he turned back to head for the diner, he caught a flash of a sleek black 4x4 dual cab pickup driving down the block running parallel to Main. It was the vehicle he had been trying to find for weeks.

After doing his homework in Fort Stockton, Hector had a feeling that truck was the one he'd been seeking. The one and only truck sold on the day the woman and baby had disappeared from town. And what's more, the same 4x4 had been paid for in cash. That told the story as far as Hector was concerned. Who paid cash these days but someone on the run?

It was a thrill knowing he'd been right. The prize was within his reach. But he would not chase after any phantom trucks this morning. Too many witnesses. Too many chances for screwups.

No, Hector would bide his time. Get the job on the Bar-C. Waiting another few days, enough time to make a plan, would be smarter than rushing in.

He wouldn't call Serrano just yet, either. Hector planned on winning. And Serrano was not known as a patient man.

Chapter 14

Grace wasn't crazy about the way her clothes smelled. Sam had insisted on her wearing his younger brothers' old jacket and hat from when they'd been teenagers. The clothes were a fair fit, but the smell of moth balls was starting to make her gag.

If he'd also been able to come up with boots from his attic's trunks, she would've begged off coming to town today. But apparently boots were passed down and worn out.

She didn't like the idea of appearing so out in the open. The town was small but public. And Jose was somewhere nearby. She could imagine him breathing down her neck.

As they rode in Sam's pickup through the back streets of town, she felt sick from both the nauseating smell and from pure, dark fear. Clearing her throat, she swallowed hard—twice.

"You okay?" Sam took his foot off the gas and gazed over at her in the passenger seat. "You're not worried about leaving Mikey with my aunt June, are you?"

"Not at all. Mikey seems to love being with June. Her home, on the outskirts of town, is such a wonderful little place. So snug and cozy. I'm sure the baby will have lots of fun playing with her in the backyard and helping her bake cookies in that warm kitchen."

Sam scowled but then said gently, "Aunt June will protect him with her life. You know that, don't you?"

Amazingly enough, Grace did know that. Not sure why these wonderful people were being so kind and taking risks for them, she nevertheless appreciated it on behalf of her son. But *she* certainly didn't deserve their kindnesses.

"I know that. It's not Mikey I'm worried about. I'm just a little shaky being out in public for the first time in days."

"We won't stay outside the fence for any longer than necessary. I want to speak to my brother and then head to the Feed and Seed Store up the highway."

Nodding that she remembered why they'd come to town, Grace checked her surroundings, looking for any trouble. "I understand. It's just that I feel…Jose. Close by."

"You *feel* Serrano? Sounds a little like alternate reality to me. Do you think you two have some sort of psychic connection?"

She gritted her teeth at the remark and then proceeded to make a noise deep in her throat that sounded like a growl. *Darned man.*

Sam chuckled a little too loudly, but never stopped searching for a parking spot in back of an office building. "Just joking. Actually I was thinking the same thing. Serrano and his men must be close and giving off a huge amount of angry, negative energy.

"We won't be long," he promised.

They parked and went around to the building's side door. While taking the stairs, he was extremely quiet.

From the few things he'd said about his brother Gage, she felt sure Sam was concerned how their reunion would go. But Travis and June had been so glad to see him after all these years. She couldn't imagine that the rest of his family wouldn't react the same way.

Sam was such a decent man. Everyone who ever knew him surely could see that.

Thinking about how much she valued Sam's sterling character, Grace realized she had become a jumble of emotions. Still wound up due to last night's interlude and her growing obsession with Sam, she felt dismayed to find out that Jose, however distantly, continued to lurk in the back of her mind like a bad dream.

When she thought of Jose, her first impulse was to run. Take Mikey and run as far and as fast as she could. But when she thought of Sam, which she did more and more often these days, she began to wonder what life would be like if she could stay in one place for a while. The place didn't matter. Just anywhere she could be near Sam.

She searched his face in profile as they walked down a long hallway toward his brother's office. His jaw was tight. His eyes narrowed. His broad shoulders were high and straight.

It made her wonder what his brother Gage would be like. Should she be afraid of this upcoming meeting on Sam's account?

Sam's current attitude also made her wonder about him. Was he keeping something from her? She'd witnessed him face bullets and deadly games of high-speed chicken. But never once in her memory had she seen him so uptight.

They came to the door with a sign that simply said: Gage Chance, Private Investigations. Sam hesitated at the threshold, shooting the cuffs of his jacket as if his nerves were rubbing him raw. Then, he breathed in one time and took her by the elbow, ushering her inside.

The walls of the first room they came to were lined with stacked cardboard boxes. Old electronic equipment sat in jumbles on every surface. The room didn't seem to have a single chair or place to sit. Sam lightly tapped on an interior door and opened it without waiting to be invited to do so.

Inside this next room the walls were mostly lined with computers and peripheral equipment. A desk sat right in the middle of the disheveled wires and oddly blinking lights. A man who looked like a younger, darker version of Sam pushed back from the desk but stayed seated as they came through the door.

"Sam." The other man shot a glance in her direction, but his face never betrayed what he was feeling.

"Hello, Gage. You were expecting us?"

"Yeah. Travis said you would be coming by."

"I see. Well, this is Grace Baker." Sam turned and actually gave her a reassuring half smile. "She and her son are under my protection."

"Ma'am." Gage nodded politely in her direction but he stayed in his seat. Seemed his mother had taught him manners, too, but he was showing no mercy to his brother by standing to shake his hand.

"If you're fixing to take a poke at me," Sam began. "I'll ask her to step out until you're done."

That remark actually brought the edges of Gage's lips

up in his own shadow version of a wry smile. "Probably not necessary. I'm in no mood to smash in your face after all these years. But you still might want her outside, unless you don't mind me being frank in front of your witness."

"Say what you need to say." Sam spread his feet and put his hands on his hips as if he was still expecting a punch in the mouth. "I didn't come to start up an old argument, brother. I came to see for myself how you're doing and to ask for a favor."

Gage's expression looked flustered for a second, then he turned to her. "Would you like to sit down? This may take a few moments."

Blinking against the roomful of testosterone-filled tension, Grace located a single chair against the back wall and slid into it. She put her hands in her lap and held her breath.

But the next words out of Gage's mouth surprised her.

Pushing to a standing position behind his desk, he held out his hand, palm up, toward his brother. "You never came back, Sam. Not once in all these years. And you promised."

Sam's shoulders twitched. "You're a P.I. You could've found me—come to me if you needed help. Travis knew where I was. Besides, it doesn't look like you've turned out so bad. I understand your business is booming."

Gage lowered his chin as though he'd taken a blow. "There's more to life than business. We haven't been able to get a line on Cami. Not in all these years of trying. And now Colt."

"What about Colt. Where is he?"

Gage shrugged a shoulder. "We're not sure. He took off without a word just like you did."

Sam shook his head for a moment, then seemed to

shake past it as he continued, "I didn't come to rehash old times, Gage. You know why I had to leave."

"Damn it!" Gage slammed his fist down on the desk. "That's bull and *you* know it. Nobody blamed you. Not one person. Least of all your family."

Sam heaved a deep sigh. "We'll do this another day. I'm still not ready to have it out with you. At least not right now."

His brother slumped down into the desk chair. "All right. Fine. What do you need?"

"Grace and her baby are being stalked by a Mexican drug lord. A very powerful drug lord."

Gage nodded. "Jose Serrano. I read the online newspaper accounts of his trial and escape when Travis told me you'd come to Chance to hide out on the old homestead."

Sam began to pace in the small space before Gage's desk. "There has to be a leak somewhere in law enforcement. His men have been showing up no matter what precautions I take."

"So you came to Chance for a showdown?"

"No!" Sam swung back and leaned on his brother's desk. "I came home because I thought Grace and Mikey would be safest here. I…we can protect her best on the ranch."

"You know everyone in town will help in any way they can."

"I'm counting on that. But right now I'm hoping you have a small thirty-eight I can borrow. For Grace."

On hearing her name, Grace sat straighter and looked up at the two men from under the brim of the stinky hat. Sam hadn't told her they were coming to borrow a handgun.

Gage threw her a sideways glance. "You think that's

smart? A pistol shouldn't be in the hands of anyone who doesn't know how to use it. Especially not with kids in the house."

She bristled and was ready to defend herself. But Sam got to it first.

"She's learning. And she's a danged good shot. I'll take all the precautions necessary for Mikey."

Gage tilted his head to study his brother. Sam stood ramrod straight under the scrutiny.

"Okay. If you say so." Gage turned, went to a wall safe Grace hadn't noticed before and removed a gun that fit in the palm of his hand. "How about this? Semiautomatic Glock seventeen. Fairly lightweight. But it still has enough firepower to stop a man before he gets too close. A female cop I know kept this one in her purse as a backup."

Sam took the gun. "Ammo?"

Gage returned to his desk, opened a drawer and pulled out a box. "Here you go."

"Thanks." Sam pocketed both the gun and the ammo. "One more favor?"

His brother raised an eyebrow but then nodded. "Sure. Whatever."

"I saw a new pharmacy across the street on our way in. Need to run an errand over there, but I don't want Grace out on the street. And I don't want her to wait alone in the car. Okay if she waits here? I'll only be ten minutes."

"Well, I don't know. She won't be any trouble, will she?" Gage's tone was obviously teasing or Grace might've started throwing her own punches. Then Gage sat back down in his chair and stared quietly up at his brother.

Sam never cracked a smile, ignoring the little joke as he turned to the door. "Thanks."

The next thing she knew, Sam was gone and she was alone with a man she knew almost nothing about. A man who didn't seem very happy to be a babysitter for a grown woman who stunk like a garbage dump and was being stalked by a drug lord.

"Can I get you something, Grace? Water? Coffee? Maybe a soda from the machine?"

"No, thanks. I'm fine."

Gage leaned his elbows on the desk and studied her for a moment. "How about you take off my old work hat so we can talk? I can store that and the coat in the other room if you like."

She stripped down to her own clothes, grinning sheepishly at the observant man as she went. Pulling open the door, she gratefully tossed the offensive hat and coat on a nearby stack of books.

"Thanks." After closing the door, she sat back down in the chair, facing him. "So, do you have many clients that come to this office? That other room doesn't exactly look…uh…welcoming."

Gage actually smiled. The first real smile she'd seen on the man's face. "If you didn't notice on the way in, Chance is not the easiest place to reach. The Bar-C does have an airstrip, but there's no commercial transportation for a hundred miles. The answer is no, no one comes here. I go to them if necessary. Besides, most of my business is done online." He waved an arm around at all the electronics.

"You must have a hard time keeping up with everything."

Gage blinked at her then frowned as he looked

around the room. "I'm thinking of hiring someone to help out with the…organization. But it's not easy to find anyone with the right qualifications who wants to live in a place so remote."

"I can understand that." But she was beginning to find the isolation and the small-town feel of the place very comforting.

Silence fell between them. She was tempted to ask about Sam, but decided she had better stay neutral. Asking just seemed too nosy.

"Do you live on the ranch?" It was the best small talk she could come up with on short notice.

"No. I live in a boarding house. Right up the street. It's fine for right now."

Grace had an inkling of something he'd left unsaid. So she tried to ease a little more information from the man. But she was beginning to feel like a reporter hot on a story.

"Don't you care for the ranch?"

Gage chuckled under his breath. "I like the ranch and the stock just fine. Every spring I help out with the cutting and spring ranching chores. In fact, it's that time of year again and I'll be staying on the ranch for the next few weeks."

"Oh." Suddenly it occurred to her that he might've been planning to stay at his old home. "Do you want to stay with us while you're working? I guess you know there's plenty of room."

A sudden sadness came into Gage's eyes. "That old house holds too many unhappy memories. For all of us. No thanks. Besides, I already have a house on the ranch where I stay while I'm working there. Built it myself for my new bride. About six years ago."

"I didn't know you were married."

"My wife…passed away. About six months after we were married. Right before the house was finished." Gage stood and faced the lone window to the street.

"I'm so sorry. Does Sam know?"

Without turning, Gage said, "I doubt it. But then it's hard to tell with Sam. He didn't show up for either Travis's or my wedding. In fact, he didn't even bother to show up at his own father's funeral."

Intrigued, Grace tried probing a little bit further. "Do you think that's because Sam was still angry with his father? He told me his old man was hard on him while he was growing up."

"Maybe." Gage returned to his desk. "But I think the more likely reason was because Dad died in prison."

"What?" Grace was shocked by the idea.

"You didn't know?"

"No—Sam…Sam never said anything."

Gage sat heavily into his desk chair. "I guess I shouldn't have said anything, either, then. It's hard explaining to people how your father died while serving time for murdering your mother."

"Really?" She hadn't had an opportunity to fully process the first shock before he'd issued the next one, so she couldn't help the comments. "How do you cope with it?"

"Not well. But then I never believed my father killed my mother. He wasn't an easy man. But he was no killer."

At a loss for words, Grace leaned back in her chair and tried to breathe evenly. In her head she worked to put Sam's steady personality and basic goodness together with his background. But she was having trouble with the two divergent components to one man.

Had Sam left because of the murder of his mother?

Or because of his father? Thinking back to the two brothers' earlier conversation about something not being Sam's fault, Grace felt she was still missing a piece of vital information.

None of this was any of her business. Despite her wild fantasies of starting a new life, she and Sam were going to become *temporary* lovers. And as soon as she had all the knowledge she needed, plus a little money set aside, she and Mikey would be running again. Leaving all the people who were coming to mean something to her, especially Sam, safely behind.

Yet she was growing more and more curious about the first man to almost make her forget her own past. And she intended to help him by finding a way inside his defenses. One way or the other.

Chapter 15

Driving to the Feed and Seed Store, Sam's skin began to crawl. Something was not right.

Grace had been too quiet since they'd left Gage's office. Maybe she felt the same strange sensation as he did. It was as if Jose Serrano followed right behind them. Sam checked the rearview mirror once more. Nothing. In fact, except for whatever was going on at the diner today, the whole town seemed deserted.

After parking in back of the store, he went around to open the door for her. "Let's go. I'd like to get this done as quickly as possible."

She swiveled and slid to the ground, grimacing. "We could skip it."

"We're here. Come on."

He reached over, taking the brim of her hat and jerking it down to cover her eyes. Then he pulled the collar of the oversize coat up to almost meet the hat. Very little of Grace's face or neck showed. But when he surveyed the disguise a little closer, he discovered nothing could cover the feminine form below the coat. The rounded hips. The long slender legs. It was all he could do to turn away and lead her into the store.

"I can't see."

"I'll help you walk until I can check things out." He slid his arm around her waist and cautioned her when they reached the back stairway.

Sneaking onto the empty loading dock, Sam gave the place a once-over for customers before going inside the store's interior. He spotted one other man besides the two guys who were obviously feed store employees. But that one customer was someone he knew from his distant past. Someone he could trust with their lives.

He walked right up the aisle toward him while Grace trailed behind, hanging on to the hem of his coat. "Sheriff McCord, do you remember me?"

McCord, who must have been sixty by now, turned from reading a label and studied him over the rim of his glasses. "Yep. I suppose I do, Chance. Hard to forget the oldest son of the most powerful family in the county. Your father hired me, remember? Nearly thirty years ago now."

"I remember." He also remembered that it was McCord who had arrested his father for the murder of his mother. "You still the sheriff?"

Sam felt no animosity toward the sheriff. It had looked to the whole world like his father had committed the crime. After all these years, Sam wasn't so sure.

"That would be right." The sheriff tilted his head to study Grace, who was covered head to toe, but he kept on talking to Sam. "I heard you were a Marshal— working for the United States government."

"That would be right."

After throwing the sheriff's own words back at him, Sam reached around and pulled the old hat off Grace's head. Her long, honey-blond hair cascaded down her shoulders and her beautiful whiskey-colored eyes blinked against the daylight.

"And this is Grace Baker. She and her son are under my protection."

Grace gave the sheriff a tentative smile and then looked to Sam for reassurance.

"This is Sheriff Austin McCord, Grace. He's been the law in this county for almost as long as I can remember."

"Nice to meet you, Sheriff." She stuck out her hand and the sheriff took it in his with a smile.

"Ma'am."

Sam could barely keep still, as he was starting to itch with apprehension. "I'd like a word, Sheriff. Just as soon as I get someone to help Grace try on boots. I'll be right there."

Leading her down the aisles toward the work boots, he signaled a clerk that she needed help. "You can try on boots by yourself for a few minutes, right?"

"I think I can manage."

"Just tell the clerk you need Western boots. They have a higher heel."

"You mean I shouldn't buy ankle-high boots? I like the looks of those better."

Sam shook his head and worked to keep the grin off his face. "I doubt that they even carry Western ankle boots in this store. You'll want *Western riding boots.*"

After he spoke to the clerk and was sure the man knew what to let her try on, Sam made his way back to the sheriff. He informed McCord about Jose Serrano's vendetta and gave him a sketch of Grace's background.

"Why would a desperado like Serrano be so interested in this Baker woman?" The sheriff scratched his head under the hat he perpetually wore. "She's already testified against him. Making an example of her now seems useless."

"She's the mother of his son. His only son as far as we can tell."

"I see. Well, that changes things, don't it? For a man from his culture, a son is everything."

"Yeah. I'm trying to keep them out of sight behind the ranch boundaries—at the old homestead. And…"

McCord interrupted him. "You don't have any trouble going back into that house, son? Some people wouldn't want anything to do with the place where their mother was murdered."

"Sheriff." Sam cleared his throat and lowered his voice. "If you remember, my brothers and I lived there for several years after the…that happened. It's just a house. The house where I grew up."

The sheriff didn't look convinced, but he lifted his chin, put his hands on his hips and straightened up. "What can I do for you?"

"Just keep an eye out here in town. You see any strangers, let me know."

"I'll do it."

Sam nodded and turned to head in Grace's direction. Then he stopped and shifted back. "What's going on down at the diner today? Lots of traffic."

"I understand Steel Brothers Contractors are hiring extra men for the Chance spring cutting. One of my deputies is directing traffic and watching for any trouble. You could probably check with Travis to be sure."

"Thanks. I'll do that. See any strangers in the bunch looking for work?"

The sheriff screwed up his mouth in thought. "No, can't say I have. I'll inquire. But as far as I've noticed, the ranch hands applying are men who've been working round here for other spreads—or they're the usual roving cowpokes we see every year."

"Thanks, Sheriff. That's good to hear." Sam turned and waved a hand as he made his way to Grace.

"How's the baby doing?"

Grace swiveled under her seat belt to check on Mikey in his car seat in the back. "He's sound asleep. He likes riding in the truck and I think he's worn out from playing with June. Will it take very long to drive us home?"

They'd only picked up her son from Sam's aunt ten minutes ago. But they were already outside of town and Sam was driving through afternoon shadows toward the ranch.

"Not long," he said quietly. "Another fifteen minutes or so. We'll be there in plenty of time to fix supper."

She pushed the smelly hat on the floor and leaned her head against the headrest, closing her eyes. It was only then, several minutes after the fact, that she realized what she'd said. She'd called Sam's old place *home*. Really? Did she actually think of the ranch that way now? This soon? She wasn't even truly convinced that Sam himself thought of the ranch as home.

Confused by her own thoughts, Grace's mind wandered back to the last time she'd believed she had a *home*. One of the worst nights of her life.

She'd already been kidnapped and held by Jose and his gang for two weeks. They'd drugged her. Starved her. Beaten her. She remembered hanging on to her sanity by a single thread. And that one slim lifeline was the naive idea that her parents were desperately raising money or doing whatever it took to bring her home.

Absently folding her arms across her chest in what would normally be a protective movement, she kept her eyes closed and fell back in time to that night.

"Please release me," she'd begged Jose. "Let me go home."

He'd laughed in her face. "You still believe those people you call parents care about you? You have no home. Not like you imagine."

Pulling her close, close enough that she smelled the alcohol on his breath, Jose kissed her on the lips. Her hands were still tied behind her back and she was too weak to resist.

"Pretty little girl," he'd cooed. "You play nice with me and I'll be nice in return. But first you need to accept the truth. Your parents don't care whether you live or die. They have refused my terms for your release."

"Refused?" Her mind was swimming with the drugs, her head light from the starvation. "No…it can't be true. They—wouldn't give up on me."

Once again he laughed, this time low and deep in his throat. "Don't worry. I've decided that *I'll* be the one to care. And once Jose Serrano cares, he will never give up on you." He ran a finger down her cheek, along her throat and down to her breastbone.

Nauseated by the words and by his touch, she gagged, but nothing was in her stomach to throw up. Jose gently shoved her back and she fell to her knees.

"*Querida,* I promise your parents will pay for causing you this pain. Meanwhile, clean yourself up. You're filthy. And I want to show you how nice I can be. But first, we must change locations. We're going to a wonderful house in the mountains. I'm going to spoil you rotten there. You'll see."

He signaled to somebody behind her back but continued speaking down to her. "Go get pretty for me. And forget about your past. Those people are dead to you. From now on, whenever you are with me, you will always have a *home*."

Grace came up out of her daydream with a start. Looking out her window, she saw that Sam was slowing for the ranch's gate. The second gate. They were almost to his old home. She checked on Mikey still sleeping in the backseat.

He was sleeping so peacefully and looked so contented that her heart twisted in a knot inside her chest. Her baby deserved a place of his own. Somehow she would have to find a way to settle down for his sake. Looking up at the house and land that she was beginning to love as they drove closer, she wondered if there would ever be a real chance for her and her son here.

"Almost there." Sam slowed and turned in front of the house. "You know, this old place is not half bad to look at. I'd almost forgotten after all these years how much I've always loved the home my ancestors built."

Well, that sounded hopeful. But Grace knew better than to start hoping for anything. Sam wouldn't want to stick around the house he'd abandoned fifteen years ago after the threat from Jose was over.

Jose. How could the threat from him ever be over? Deep down she knew better. *Once Jose Serrano cares, he will never give up on you.*

"Will you watch Mikey while I make supper?" Grace slid to the ground in front of the house.

Sam nodded to her as he reached into the backseat to

pull a groggy baby from his car seat. For some reason Grace looked tired this evening. He wished he could take her out to dinner and give her a break from reality. Help her forget—for just a little while.

He would do anything to take away the shadows sitting on her shoulder. She'd already been through so much in the past five years. He wanted to wipe away those memories and help her make new ones.

But there wasn't any way they could leave the ranch again tonight or for the next few days. They'd already taken a huge chance by staying in town so long today.

Maybe once the cowpokes began their spring cutting work and everyone was coming and going, the town would be too busy for anyone to notice them. Meanwhile he vowed to do everything within his power to take her mind off the threat.

They were safe here. And he wanted her to enjoy the time they spent together.

"Da!" Mikey suddenly was wide awake against his shoulder. "Da. Da!"

"Yeah, baby, I've got you and we're almost home." He started jiggling Mikey up and down in his arms. "Are you hungry? Mama is going to make you something to eat."

Mikey didn't look hungry. In fact, he looked as if he wanted playtime. And Sam was happy to oblige. It was the least he could do tonight for Grace.

"Let's get you changed and then we'll go play in the kitchen and watch Mama make dinner. Okay?" Sam kicked off his boots at the door and took the stairs two at a time with Mikey in his arms.

The baby was not thrilled about having his diaper changed and Sam had to chase him across the bed a couple of times. Still, he found himself chuckling at how bright the boy was about timing his escapes. Smart little kid.

When at last they made it to the kitchen, Grace was concocting a salad from the last of the fresh vegetables. "Well, hello. How are my two favorite men getting along?"

"We have clean diapers—after a few tussles. And we're ready to play. Got any suggestions?"

"Not the pans and spoons, please. I don't think my head can take the noise tonight."

Concerned, Sam went to stand beside Grace. "You have a headache?"

With a glance that nearly sent him to his knees, she murmured low, "I'm just a little hungry. It's nothing that should slow us down—later."

He'd forgotten the real reason they'd gone to town, but now his body remembered every promise, every urge, all loud and clear and rushing through his veins. "Did you bring the…uh…our purchases inside?"

"Everything but the gun you borrowed. Where is that?"

Forcing his libido back down so he could manage an answer, he said, "I stashed it in a weapons safe under the truck's front seat. We'll practice loading and firing tomorrow and find a place to keep it in the house that'll be the safest."

All of a sudden Mikey decided he'd been holding still for long enough while the two adults talked. He let out a screech that could've been heard clear out in the barn.

"Put him on the floor." Grace laughed and nodded to her bag in the corner. "There's a ball in there. Try rolling it to him."

Doing as instructed, Sam was amazed at how the baby could play ball and roll it right back to him.

"Mikey couldn't do this when I last saw the two of you in Denver."

"Babies grow fast, Sam. Blink and they're going off to college."

The idea of Mikey growing up and moving out on his own threw him for a minute or two. He didn't want to miss all the changes. Didn't want to wonder what new things the baby had learned while he wasn't looking.

He'd grown fond of Mikey. More than fond, he supposed.

"Okay, Mikey's dinner is ready and ours will be done in a second." Grace's voice brought him back from a very bleak future. "Let's get our boy into his high chair."

Our boy. Was that what he *really* wanted? He'd developed some different attitudes since meeting Grace. But had he grown so much over the past few months that he genuinely cared about the little guy enough to change his whole life?

He'd never imagined that he would be a father. His own father had made a terrible model to follow. From the time Sam turned twelve, the two of them had argued bitterly, right up until the day his father had been arrested.

Lost in his thoughts, Sam had been slow to move, so Mikey grabbed hold of his shirt sleeve and managed to make it to a standing position on his own two feet. "Mama!"

"Good point, son. Mama wants us to get a move on. Supper's served. I hear you."

Pulling Mikey into his arms, Sam swung him into the high chair. Then he straightened up and turned to help Grace. But she still stood in the same place and now was dabbing at her eyes with a paper towel.

"What is it? Something wrong?"

She shook her head sadly. "Mikey's never said 'Mama' like he knew what it meant before."

Sam put his arms around her shoulder. "Well, that's nothing to cry about. It's great. Didn't you just say…"

"Oh, Sam, what if Jose somehow gets to him? What if we can't protect him? Mikey will grow up and never know me. He's so young he won't remember his own mother."

"We won't let that happen. I swear to you, Grace. As long as I'm alive, Serrano will never put his hands on this child."

After a moment Grace dried her tears and they managed to have a quiet, almost solemn supper. When they finished the dishes, she insisted Mikey needed a bath before bedtime and carried him up the stairs.

At a loss and feeling odd, like he had no roots, Sam took off up the stairs, too. But instead of joining them in the bathroom, he told Grace where he was headed and then made his way to the attic. He was looking for something that reminded him of his own mother.

He remembered her clearly. Though sometimes it was hard to picture her face after all these years. But he didn't want a photograph of her. No, something else would bring her memory back in a much better way.

It took him a few minutes to find the object he was seeking. Under a load of old drapes and covered in dust, he found the toy box that his grandfather had made by hand for him so many years ago.

He dusted off the familiar wooden top, carved into the shapes of balls, horses and lassos. As he opened the lid, he remembered his mother packing toys into it for the last time. His youngest brother, Denton, had recently ridden in his first horse show and suddenly dropped the toys of his babyhood, wanting to be more grown-up like his older brothers. And his mother hadn't figured her new baby daughter would be terribly interested in boys' toys.

But as Sam reached inside the box, the first thing he came to was the old bathtub yellow duck. He distinctly remembered Cami as a baby, playing with it in the tub. Maybe Mikey would like playing in the tub, too. He set it aside.

Really looking for the baby books that his mother used to read to him at bedtime, Sam searched through the box. But memories assaulted him with every cracked or chipped toy. Mind pictures of himself, Travis, Gage and Colt playing ball. Or sitting on the great room floor with a new set of trains. Christmas mornings. Easter egg hunts.

And with every memory, his mother's face became clearer. Until she was so real, he could almost smell her shampoo.

His hand landed on the child-size stirrups that his grandfather had designed for him as a boy. But it wasn't the memory of himself riding for the first time that came to mind. Instead he could hear his mother's words as she handed them to him for the last time.

"Be a good oldest brother, Sam," she'd said firmly. "I'm counting on you to teach Denton to ride. I know it seems like a pain now, you're a full-fledged teenager and think you're too grown up. But your baby brother wants to be just like you. He wants to do everything you do. Teach him. Work with him. I'm swamped, what with expecting the new baby."

His mother had kissed him tenderly on the forehead then, the same way she had when he'd been a little kid. "I'm putting you in charge. Watch out for Denton. Don't let anything happen to him."

Sam stared down at the stirrups in his hand. His vision was blurred, though the memories were as clear as a summer Texas day.

"Sam?" Grace's voice broke through the pain. "What's the matter?"

Rubbing the heels of his palms across his eyes, he put the stirrups down and stood. "It's nothing."

She gently placed her fingers to his cheek. "Tell me."

He turned away from her touch. "I've been thinking maybe I'll ask Travis to send over a couple of hands to stand watch on the house round the clock."

"What? Why? I thought you and I could handle it."

The cold bore into his chest. "I can't do this. I shouldn't do this. It's too important. Just like the last time. I'll screw it up again."

"What are you saying? You don't screw up. You're the one in charge. You save people."

Taking her by the shoulders, he gave her a shake—he had to make her see. "I killed my little brother, Grace. By screwing up. Denton is dead. And he died while I was in charge."

Chapter 16

"Oh, Sam." In her gut Grace was sure that whatever he'd just remembered, however bad it could be, *this* was the cause of all his sad looks. And the reason for the rift between him and Gage. *This* memory was bound to be the basis for him not coming home in the past fifteen years.

She caught his arm and dragged him over to an ancient rattan bench. "Sit. Tell me the whole story. Make me understand why you feel so guilty."

"Where's Mikey? Is he all right?" Sam absently sat beside her.

"Mikey's sound asleep. A full tummy and a warm bath did it. He should be fine until morning."

She touched Sam's chin and made him look at her. "Stop stalling. You're important to me. What hurts you, hurts me. I want to know what happened."

"I...don't know where to start."

"At the beginning. Or on the day that things changed."

Sam leaned his elbows on his knees, hung his head and stared at the floor. "Everything changed the day my mother died. None of us has ever been the same. My father and my youngest brother are gone for good now and my little sister is…" His voice turned hoarse and he coughed.

Grace kept her own voice even, trying not to sound either sympathetic or accusing. "I know your father died in prison while serving time for your mother's murder. And I remember you telling me the story about your little sister being kidnapped. It seemed like a heck of a lot of misery and trouble for one family. What happened to Denton?"

"It *was* a lot of misery—collapsing around us all at once. And most of it was my fault. After my father first went to jail, I stepped into the role he had always wanted for me. At nineteen I was head of the Bar-C ranch."

Shaking his head, Sam continued slowly, "Our extended family, all the aunts and cousins, wanted to split us kids up. The plan was for every relative to take a kid into their home, but none of them lived in Chance. Travis and I rebelled against the idea. I was adamant that the family stay together. I was so full of myself and so angry at my mother and father for leaving us alone that I refused to let well-meaning relations come to our aid."

He stopped for a second, breathed. The memories seemed to be too much for him to take, but he soldiered on. "Travis was old enough to stand beside me on refusing a split. We didn't want the family broken up any more than necessary."

"I can understand that. But…"

"I was wrong. I couldn't handle it. I shouldn't have tried. I hated running the ranch. It consumed my every waking moment. And trying to be sure that the little ones were well taken care of weighed heavily on my mind. So months later when my mother's sister offered to take Cami into her home, Travis and I readily agreed. What did we teenage boys know about raising a four-year-old girl?"

"Sam, that wasn't your…"

"I was in charge." He'd said the words so forcefully that Grace closed her mouth and just listened. "I had made arrangements for our housekeeper to stay on and saw to it that we were fed and had clothes to wear. I could've found someone to come and take care of Cami, as well. It turned out my aunt June made sure Travis graduated from high school and that the younger boys kept up with their grades. Maybe she…"

His words scattered and dropped off, leaving Grace to imagine he must be thinking not only about his sister but also what had happened to his youngest brother.

"There was a lot of anger in our house in those days," he said. "Besides being mad at my parents, I was furious with myself for letting Cami out of my sight. But somehow we managed to get by like that for a couple of years. Each of us living our own miserable lives. Except for Travis. He insisted on helping me run the place. He was good with the ranch hands. Great with the paperwork. All the stuff I hated.

"Eventually he took the bulk of the work off my shoulders." Sam looked up at the ceiling, still not seeing her.

He seemed lost in his misery. "I guess Travis was meant to run the ranch in the first place. I should've let him take charge earlier. Later, after Denton died and I left town, Travis finished raising our brothers and he made the Bar-C into the showplace it is now. I could've..."

As his words ran out again, Grace felt she should break in. Tell him that it wasn't his fault. Not everyone was cut out to do every job in this world. And he'd faced more tragedy as a young man, no more than a boy really, than anyone should ever have to take.

But what she said instead was, "How did Denton die? You've never said."

"I've never said because I haven't talked about it. Not to anyone. Not ever."

Pressing his lips together, Sam remained silent for a long time. Just when she was about to give up, stop his reminiscing and beg him to stop thinking about what couldn't be changed, he finally began his story.

"Denton was eleven. He came to me one day and asked if he could help out by joining the ranch hands who were working in one of our westernmost pastures. I was too busy to pay much attention. Other responsibilities seemed a lot more important. I told him yes just to get rid of him."

Sam stood and began to pace. "What was I thinking? An eleven-year-old kid has no place out on the range without supervision. At the very least, I should've sent someone with him."

She saw him tense as the painful memories stabbed into his mind yet again. He didn't deserve to do this to himself. No matter what had happened. But how could she be the best help?

"Sam." She stood and went to his side. Stood in his way and made him quit pacing and look at her. "Tell me all of it. You have to get everything, every single memory, out in the open now before it eats you alive."

Grace heard her own words, knew somewhere deep

in her psyche that she should be telling herself the exact same things, but *this* moment belonged to Sam. She could bury hers deep inside the same way she'd been doing for years.

Taking his hands in hers, she waited and held her breath. He shrugged, tried to look away.

"Please." Tugging at his hands, she forced him to focus back on her face. "It's me. You know I won't judge."

Swallowing hard, he gazed into her eyes and began, "It was a stupid mistake. A kid's mistake. Denton wanted to join up with the hands who'd been stringing fence wire. I guess he thought he could take a shortcut to reach them before lunch by racing his horse over a seldom-used pasture."

Sam stopped and narrowed his eyes at her. "Even expert riders need to take it slow when riding on uneven ground that isn't familiar. Remember that."

She simply nodded. Afraid to stop him by making any comments.

"The tragedy must have begun when his horse stumbled into a prairie dog hole. We're not entirely sure of the sequence of events after that. Apparently Denton tried to rein in the horse, but the animal had twisted his leg and may have been spooked. By a rattler. Or maybe an armadillo. Anyway, somewhere along the line, the horse reared, threw my brother and landed on him. The horse survived. My little brother didn't. A grown man might've lived through such a fall, but not a kid."

The tears in Sam's eyes were too much for Grace. She stopped him from speaking by cupping his cheek.

"You weren't any more than a kid yourself. Stop taking all the blame for an accident you couldn't control."

He looked as if he wanted to pull away, hunker down into his pain.

So she went on, trying to make him see. "Even if you'd been there, he might've still died. Isn't that right? An accident can happen at any time."

She lowered her voice to a whisper. "You've already paid for the minor mistake of being young and in way over your head. You've paid many times. Think of all the people you've saved since then. In the army. As a Marshal. The people who might've died if not for you."

"You don't understand."

Now *her* eyes were misting over. In that instant she would've said anything, done anything, to take away his hurt. He had already been so good to her and Mikey. He'd literally saved their lives and their hearts. He didn't deserve the pain of facing his demons alone.

"You seriously believe I don't know about guilt?" she asked. "That I've just been the victim in my life?"

"No." He'd said the word too forcefully. Of course he thought that. Everyone thought that.

But she let it slide. This was about him.

"Well, I do understand," she insisted. "What I don't understand is why you can't see how much you've already given back. Don't you know that Mikey and I might be dead if not for you?"

"Maybe."

"Definitely. You need to accept that you did what you could and pitched in when it was needed the most. You gave Travis the time and training he had to have in order to take over the ranch. He was too young when your mother died to step right up, but you did. You didn't turn and run, Sam. You stayed and tried your best."

"I suppose. But..."

Seizing the moment and interrupting him, she

screwed up her courage and tugged at his neck, bringing his lips close enough for a kiss. He shut up but jerked upward, just enough to remind her that she was enormously vulnerable. What would she do if he pulled away?

She prayed. Like she hadn't prayed since the kidnapping.

At that moment the look in his eyes changed. And the air in the room changed. Her whole world tilted on its axis.

He was hot for her. The sadness in his eyes had ignited to flames. And his obvious lust succeeded in turning her into a puddle of jelly.

She couldn't fix everything with a kiss. Couldn't take away his guilt or wave a wand and let him have a do-over on his youth. She couldn't even give him the promise of a brighter future.

But hopefully she *could* make him forget for one night. Together they would soar, high above the pain and the memories. Just for one night. Just for Sam's sake.

Before she could move, though, he breached the void between them, leaned down and opened his mouth over hers. Then deepened the kiss. Oh, yeah. His mouth was amazing. Hot. Wild. Hungry.

His hands went to her hair, pulling her close as he sensually ran his fingers through the strands. The promise of the night of her dreams was there. In his touch. In his taste.

Clinging to him, she felt his body tighten, growing hard against her belly. The heat between them was setting her on fire.

She'd waited her whole life for a night like this. But believed she would never have one since Jose had ruined

her for most men. But not for Sam. She needed this night
every bit as much as Sam did. Maybe more.

So when he lifted his head and leaned back, she panicked. Made a squeak of protest.

"Easy there." He scooped her up in his arms and held
her close to his chest. "Where are…?"

His voice was so raspy she could barely understand.
"For God's sake, Grace. Where'd you put the protection?"

Sam's heart pounded nearly out of his chest as he
carried her down one flight of stairs, retrieving the box
from the master bedroom. Mikey was sleeping peacefully and Sam wanted to be sure he stayed that way.

He carried Grace and the box into his old bedroom,
carefully laying her on his bed. He was unsure of how
to proceed. But when she looked up at him and smiled,
the doubts fled and everything was a go.

As he began to undress her, he marveled at how
lovely she was. It had been a long, very long, time since
he'd made love to a woman. So long he couldn't remember the face or the name.

Now, Grace filled his head. Visions of her and his
growing hunger. Suddenly he wanted to consume every
bit of her. Wanted to inhale her, surround her, learn the
details of what made Grace.

She'd been through a lot physically and emotionally,
and he wanted this to be good. Nonthreatening and skill-
ful. Noticing how his hands shook as he unbuttoned her
blouse and lowered her jeans' zipper, he tried not to ac-
cidently touch her wonderful, warm body. Not yet.

He'd spent months battling this desire, but for Grace's
sake he had to be strong. And gentle. Patient.

Slowly, so slowly he felt like screaming, he dragged

the jeans down her hips and off. Then he helped her shrug out of the blouse, until she was left in bra and panties.

Only then did he feel too well covered. But with two quick jerks of cloth, his own shirt disappeared.

The intensity in her eyes as she gazed at his bare chest and farther on down to his waistband mesmerized him, making him fumble fingered and slow. When she impatiently reached for his belt buckle, he froze.

As her warm fingers slowly lowered his zipper and pushed at his jeans and underwear, he sucked in his ab muscles and forgot to breathe. Then the tables turned and it was her breath that caught when he sprung free of the cloth restraints. The sounds she made thankfully woke him up enough to kick the jeans aside.

Lying on her back on the bed, she was quiet as she watched him strip. What a tantalizing picture she made. The thing he couldn't figure out was how to go slow and fast at the same time.

Desperate to make this good for her, he fought to stem his recklessness. Nice and easy. He wanted it better than good. The best. Because he knew that's how making love with her would be for him.

Patience.

Leaning closer, he pressed a knee into the bed beside her. The warmth of her hip connected to his thigh and the physical connection seemed to overpower any last-minute jitters. From both of them.

She reached out to him again, and he found himself straddling her hips without missing a step. The whole room was electric with anticipation as she took both of his hands with her own and placed them to her breasts.

Wanting more than just a touch through the material of her bra, Sam reached around her back and, sight unseen, undid the hook. For a second he was surprised he could remember that youthful trick from so long ago, but the growing heat in her eyes cleared his mind of everything but pleasing her.

He slowly peeled the lace away from her breasts, revealing the most enticing sight. The hard tips of her nipples were nearly purple. Flushed with desire. Losing a little control, he couldn't help it. Touch would not be nearly enough. Lowering his head, he drew a nipple into his mouth and rolled his tongue over the tip.

She arched and squirmed under him. "Oh, Sam. That's so good. Your mouth is so hot. Feels…I…I…"

Wild for her, he sucked and laved, nipped and then soothed. Her moans and moves fed his hunger.

Easy does it.

Kissing his way up her chest and neck, he found her lips and feasted on them. She clutched at his arms and dug her nails into his shoulders.

This was going way too fast. She'd sent him to a level of arousal that neared the danger point. He pulled up and leaned back a little, staring down at the most beautiful sight he could ever remember. Grace, eyes wide with passion, licked her lips and murmured about her needs.

"Please hurry," she managed in the most erotic whisper.

Their gazes locked, and what he saw was not purely passion. There, in those eyes the shade of rare bourbon, he saw trust. And it amazed him. Humbled him.

Changed him, in subtle ways he could not have expected.

Once more she took one of his hands and drew it down her body to the small scrap of material at the juncture of her thighs. Apparently Grace wasn't happy with the pace he'd been setting.

If he hadn't been so close to a dangerous edge, he might've smiled at the idea. Instead he rubbed their joined hands against the wet cloth, then let her fingers go, urging her with silent moves to open her legs. She relaxed, her legs opening wider. And then he cupped her, caressing and enticing.

Sliding a finger underneath the material's edge, he skimmed lightly across her damp curls.

"Sam." She sighed his name, but he heard the tension building in her voice.

The fire inside him threatened to take him far too soon. It was one thing to go easy, and quite another to drive them both insane.

"Take the panties off," he ordered in a shaky voice.

She scrambled to remove them as he fumbled with the condom box. His fingers seemed twice their normal size and too clumsy for the job. When at last he had a foil packet in hand, he knew he was sunk.

Tossing it at her, he begged, "Open it and cover me."

Her fingers shook, too. But she ripped it open with her teeth. Then while making little whimpering noises, she unrolled it over him. When done, she flopped back down on her back with a nervous little laugh and watched him carefully.

"Oh, no, you don't," he said with his own chuckle. "You've gotten us this far."

Grabbing her up against his chest, he rolled them both over. She lay sprawled across him, breathing heavily and sounding more tense and desperate than ever.

"*You* do the work." His voice sounded reedy and too damned shaky. "Set the pace for us. It's your night, sweetheart, I give you my body. Take us where you want us to go."

He helped her sit up, her legs straddling his hips. "Sam, I don't know how to do this."

Finding her core, he checked her readiness. Wet. And so hot he thought her skin might spontaneously combust.

"Go with your instincts."

Pressing her lips together with determination, Grace came up on her knees. She had no idea what she was doing but she wouldn't let him down. She wouldn't let *herself* down. This was all new and Sam had given her a gift she wanted to earn.

He helped her by fitting his erection to the exact right spot on her body. The spot that was the most sensitive and now was aching. Slowly she began lowering her buttocks onto him. Slow. Careful.

"You're incredible, sweetheart. You feel so good."

Good Lord, the freedom he'd given her. The *power.* She'd never felt anything like it.

Sam laid back, sensually watching her every move with dark passion in his eyes. Just his expression drove her to a brand-new level of arousal.

Suddenly empowered and emboldened, she leaned forward and stopped the movement of her hips. Easing upward, she kissed his chest and then gazed into his eyes.

"Grace."

She didn't move. Not one muscle.

"Gracie, you're killing me here." Those might've been his words, but he never moved a muscle, either.

He froze, waiting for her decision. Her move was first? No matter what? The man was remarkable. She would never forget this—or him.

Taking pity, and needing to ease the tension curling tight inside her own body, she sat back up and let him slide in all the way. Sam had been right. She felt incredible.

The moment she seated herself and rocked her hips, he groaned and thrust upward. Suddenly everything was a whirlwind of movement. In and out. Slow than fast. Together they set a pace, then changed it at will.

Every move taught her something new about her own body. The powerful sensations he created within her drove her to a torrid kind of pleasure she had never known existed.

Finally time ceased to exist. Thought ceased to exist.

She could only feel. The momentum built deep in her core. The inevitable loomed larger with every relentless move.

Nearly blind and deaf with need, at last she had no delaying tactic left and dove over the edge. Fierce and razor-edged, her freefall was so intense that she couldn't help crying out with the sheer joy of it.

Sam soon joined her, arching his back as he found his own release with a shout.

Gasping for breath, she collapsed over him as their bodies pulsed together with the all-consuming wave. Laughing and crying at the same time, she wished the rush could never end.

That real life would never intrude.

Chapter 17

The moment he could breathe again and make his limbs do as he demanded, Sam rolled them both over, keeping her snuggled in his arms. She sighed and burrowed closer.

Lying on his side in the darkness, he reveled in the warm feel of the woman beside him and dwelt on the sensations still pulsating through his body. She'd been incredible. They were amazing together. He couldn't have asked for a better lover.

But what was he to do with these emotions? It felt as if what they'd done was not just sex but something a damned site more.

He should never have agreed to, or maybe in truth *suggested,* this. He should've known better. The rolling wave of feelings for her and her son had apparently messed with his mind.

Now what?

As she scooted her bottom against his groin, what he wanted next was all too obvious. The need to be inside her again, to kiss her into passion and take them both right back to those fireworks, threatened to ruin his long-running and up-to-now *famous* control.

Aw hell. What was he thinking? His control where she was concerned had already left the building. Gone the way of his many vows to do nothing but keep her safe. And what's more, along with his loss of control, he'd probably also lost his job. This little dip into a personal quest, like something out of King Arthur's tales, was bound to cause a bad mark on his record that might never be erased.

His job. Sam didn't give a rip about the job. He'd just been making the motions over the past couple of years anyway.

But he did care about Grace and Mikey. He would give anything to wrap them both up and carry them to a place where no one had ever heard of Serrano—or of any Mexican drug lords for that matter.

Though such a place might only be in his head. A dream world. Not reality. In real life no place would be safe. Not until Serrano was dead.

He listened to Grace breathing. Slow and steady. She'd fallen asleep cocooned in his arms.

The trust she'd given him was astounding. After all her troubles, she'd thought only of his interests.

She'd wrangled her way inside his soul and made him talk about losing his little brother. Something he hadn't done since the day Denton had died. Wide cracks in the shield of guilt he'd worn for too many years fell open, exposing the raw nerves and self-incrimination he'd lived with every day since then. It was painful to be so exposed, but necessary if he would ever lead a normal life.

And suddenly he wanted a normal life. Being with Mikey had made him hungry to be a father. Being with Grace, making love to her—loving her—was the best thing that had happened to him in…forever.

But when Serrano was no longer a threat, she'd be gone. He knew that. She'd told him often enough. And she'd proved it at least once before.

What was Sam to do to prepare himself for her departure?

Well, for one thing, he could stop thinking that far ahead and dwelling only on himself. He had bigger worries at the moment.

He believed Grace wasn't as mentally and emotionally strong as she pretended. That seemed abundantly clear to him now. She needed to spend more time with a psychiatrist. She'd only taken a few weeks during the trial to see the FBI's mental health professionals. Afterward she'd insisted that she didn't need help, swearing that having a child had changed her. Becoming a mother was all the healing necessary.

He couldn't see her as recovered. Pain and sadness continued to linger on in her eyes. It was there whenever she thought no one was looking.

When the threat from Serrano was over, getting her the help she needed would be his first priority.

Meanwhile he needed to step up his game where Serrano was concerned. Tomorrow he would call Travis and have him start closely checking every man who entered the ranch to work. He could also nail the windows shut and alarm the doors. And hide a weapon in every room he might enter.

Most of all he needed to make a new plan. A plan to

stash Mikey and Grace someplace safe while he went to Mexico in search of Serrano. The only way to end her nightmare for good was to put Serrano either behind bars—or below ground.

Grace sat at the kitchen table the morning after the most spectacular night of her life, feeding Mikey and waiting for Sam to walk back through the door. He'd said he needed to go outside to make better preparations for an attack. But that scared her, made her feel more vulnerable than ever.

Every possible emotion careened through her mind and confused her brain. In her childhood dreams, at least as much as she could remember before Jose, the morning after such a spectacular night would be reserved for cuddling and whispering words of devotion.

Sam wasn't even in the bed when she'd awoken this morning. He'd already gone downstairs to the kitchen. She'd found him drinking coffee, waiting for her and Mikey to show up. After she'd fumbled the baby into his high chair, Sam had left, saying something about calling Travis and Gage. But without a word about last night.

After last night, Sam had broken down the icy walls Jose had constructed in her mind and body, leaving her too open and...

And what? Changed. That was for sure. A little lost? Yes. But mostly, she felt deep in her bones that the strange emotion at the top of her current list had to be love.

Yeah, she was well and truly sunk. And definitely in love with Sam.

Mikey, too, had formed an attachment. In one way this would be good for the baby. Her son needed a man in his life. A good and decent man. But loving Sam could be a bad thing if the man in question didn't return their feelings. More terrible still would be if, when Jose was safely in jail, Sam went back to his job and stopped protecting them. *Forgot about them.*

Yet she didn't want to talk to him about her fears or her dreams. Couldn't think of a way of telling him how she felt. The biggest reason she'd stayed silent was to be sure he didn't start thinking she'd set out to trap him all along.

So she sat and stewed and waited.

After she finished with Mikey's breakfast. And finished washing down the mess he'd made in the kitchen. And *then* finished washing him down and changing his clothes. Grace thought she and the baby should take a little walk in the sunshine. Outside her window it seemed like a lovely spring day.

Maybe they'd find Sam nearby the house somewhere. And Mikey would love a chance to see the horses again.

Holding the baby in her arms, she stepped through the kitchen door and realized a large crowd of people had gathered down by the barns. This must be the start of what Sam had said was the Bar-C's spring cutting.

Hesitating, she drew a huge breath of air into her lungs and looked over the scene. Men were already taking the horses, both moms and babies, out of the barns and into the small fenced-off areas Sam told her were called rings or corrals.

Fascinating.

"Da!" Mikey held out his arm and pointed toward the horses.

"No, baby. I told you. It's 'horse.' Can you say *horsey?*"

"Da...da!"

When Grace finally glanced up to where her child

was pointing, she noticed Sam heading in their direction. "Ah. It is him. I sure wish you were right, Mikey. I wish he was your daddy."

Suddenly the tears backed up behind her eyes. Swallowing hard, she bit her lip and waited until Sam came closer before trying to say anything.

"What are you two doing outside?" Sam's hat was pulled low over his forehead and his voice was gruff.

"It's such a lovely day," she answered with as easy a tone as she could manage. "The flowers are blooming and there's a wonderful light breeze. We came outside to find you, hoping we could all go down to see the horses."

Sam stood silently for a moment while he screwed up his mouth as if he was considering it.

Then he turned his head back to the barns. "I suppose we could watch the foals from outside the fence while the hands parade them out of the barn. But not for long. When the real work begins, it'll be messy and..."

"And—what?"

He twisted back to her. "And lots more men will be arriving after a while. The real wranglers. I'd rather you and Mikey stay in the house out of sight when they arrive."

"Oh." He'd brought the threat from Jose back into their conversation with a thud.

The day seemed to cloud over. Flies buzzed around her face. Her morning was ruined.

"Da!" But Mikey's day still shone with possibility.

"Hey, bud. Come on over here." Grinning, Sam pulled the baby out of her embrace and sat him in the crook of his arm. "Want to walk down to see the horses with me? Looks like your mama already has her boots on and is raring to go."

The three of them started over the fields, heading toward one of the many fenced rings. Mikey babbled away, making no sense at all but enjoying himself anyway.

"I wonder when Mikey will be able to say more words. Understandable words." Sam smiled and nodded at the baby's nonsensical conversation.

"Pretty soon, I would imagine. He's already making most of his wants clear enough. And he's right where a one-year-old boy should be. At least the doctors' charts all say that."

"A year old? He can't be that old. When?"

"Tomorrow, actually. What would you think if we have a little party for him? We could invite your brother's niece and your aunt June. And I'll bake him a cake. That is if we can get hold of a cake mix and frosting. I wouldn't want to try making anything from scratch."

Sam chuckled. "I'll bet you'd be a great baker if you worked at it. Studied on it. My mom left lots of cook-books."

His good humor and trust in her competence made her smile. "Not this time, please. No one would want to take a chance on my baking. I'll practice up for the next time, though."

"Okay. We can make a quick trip into town later today. After you practice using the thirty-eight."

There he went, ruining the beautiful day again. She nodded and hung her head, watching her step through the fields.

"Are you all right?" he asked after a few silent moments.

"Sure."

As they came closer to the fence, Mikey picked up the volume of his babbling.

"The baby seems to like it here." Sam grinned as Mikey jumped excitedly in his arms. "How about the baby's mama? Have you been happy staying on the ranch, Grace? It can be, well, a little rough and isolating."

"I love it here." Oops. That may have been a bit too strong. She didn't want him to guess what she really loved was him—and that she would love any place where he went.

But Sam just nodded as he kept on watching the men work with the horses.

"How about you, Sam? Are you happy being back home? I can't imagine how you stayed away so long."

He gave her a quizzical stare. "Hadn't given it that much thought." Looking out toward the ranch hands, he added, "Times like the spring cutting were always the best on the ranch. And maybe I would like to try my hand at gentling a horse again. I used to be pretty good at it."

Exhaling a long breath, he lifted the hat off his forehead and wiped his brow with the back of his hand. "So, yeah, I guess I do miss some points about living on the ranch."

A really good sign, in Grace's opinion. If he could remember the good things over and above the bad things that had happened on the ranch, then maybe he was beginning to overcome his guilt. She hoped so. In fact, she hoped he would start loving the idea of being on the ranch again. Want to stay here for good. Getting him to settle down would be a big boon to their relationship.

If they really had a relationship. *If* it wasn't all in her mind.

"It's time to head back." Sam spoke to Mikey, "We'll come down later and visit the horses, son. After the ranch hands' work is done for the day. Right now, we need to call Auntie June. You like Auntie June, don't you?"

Instead of the tears and anger Grace had expected from her child when he moved away from the fence, Mikey smiled and patted Sam's cheek. "Dune."

"Well, I'll be darned." Sam laughed. "Guess you remember her and like her. That's my good boy. Me, too."

His good boy?

Yet another good sign in her humble opinion. He was beginning to think of Mikey in different terms than just a witness he had to protect.

Now, if only he would start thinking of her in a different, and very special new way, too.

Sighing under her breath, she quickened her step to catch up. "Why are you calling June?"

"Well, I'd originally wanted to ask her to babysit while we went to town for cake mix. But I've been thinking that over. The idea of you being off the ranch while all these unknown cowpokes are milling about town is too risky.

"Besides," he added. "I need to stick around this afternoon and work on additional security and safeguards for the house."

"Oh." Darn him. He kept taking her wonderful dreams of the two of them doing domestic things, like baking cakes and having birthday parties, and smashing them to bits with images of Jose and his men coming after them.

Sam turned to study her. "Don't look so miserable. I didn't mean we won't have a cake. I'll call June and ask her to stop at the store for a mix and then bring it out to us. You can bake the thing tonight."

"Oh! Okay, I guess that'll work."

She would rather her dreams not be interrupted by a day filled with security precautions and learning to fire a handgun. But tonight…tonight they would become closer over preparations for a party. And afterward she would find some way of seducing him back into bed.

They were good together—whether he realized it or not. And she intended to do everything in her power to remind him of that fact at every opportunity.

Bumping along in the back of an open pickup, Serrano's men Hector and Pedro were being driven to the horse barns on the Bar-C ranch.

Alone in the truckbed, Hector used the opportunity to speak to his *compañero*. "It's a good thing we've been assigned to work with the horses. Not with the cattle."

"Yes. A good thing. I don't know about cattle or sheep. I know horseflesh."

"*Si.* That's what I told them. Right after I learned a baby had been spotted in an old house near the horse barns. Maybe we'll get lucky and see some signs of his child and the mother. Keep your eyes open."

"*His?* How do you know this baby is Serrano's boy?"

Frustrated by the non-too-smart Pedro, Hector screwed up his patience one more time and said, "Good guessing. Who else would be hiding a child on the Bar-C?"

Hector openly touched the handgun he had hidden inside his denim jacket to remind Pedro of why they were really here. "We are prepared to do what is necessary."

"So soon? But you told el jefe we would wait. That we would look around and make a good plan."

"I told the boss that story to make him happy. But if we find his child, we must act fast. The lawman who hides the woman and baby is smart. Too smart. If we wait too long, he may make it impossible for us to capture them. Remember, the woman might disappear again at any moment. And the next time, the boss's contact in L.A. probably won't be able to help us find her."

Shaking his head slowly, Hector went through every scenario in his mind and decided the minute he was sure, they should act. "No, it must be done quickly. The sooner the better."

Pedro began to pout. "But I like working with horses. Can't we at least stay for the earmarking?"

"Don't be stupid." Hector nearly drew down on the idiot sitting beside him. "We're not here to work with horses. Jose Serrano does not pay top wages to horse wranglers."

"But—"

"Just shut up and do what I tell you."

"Wait. How will we get away with the baby? We didn't drive our own truck on the range."

Lifting a shoulder, Hector said, "I'll think of something. We both know how to drive and you know how to start a truck without a key. Don't you?"

"*Si,* but it's so far to the gate. What if...?"

"Maybe we would be smarter to ride horseback off the ranch. We could disappear onto the range, and it might take days for them to track us down. We'd ride into town, grab the truck and be in Mexico before they had any idea where we'd gone."

The more Hector thought about that solution, the better he liked it. Taking a baby on horseback would be no trouble.

"Hector..."

"No more conversation. We're almost there."

"Look!"

Hector turned his head in the direction where Pedro was pointing. A tall, lean man and a beautiful woman strolled across the fields toward an old farmhouse. And on the man's shoulders was a brown-skinned baby who looked to be about a year old.

Amazing. Could he really be this lucky?

Luck, nothing. Hector knew the good fortune came because he was smart. Smarter than the next guy. Maybe even smarter than Jose Serrano.

Yes. They *were* almost there.

Chapter 18

It felt like the longest day in Grace's memory. Longer than her twenty-hour labor ordeal having Mikey. *And* even longer than the weeks-long horrors at Jose's hands after the kidnapping.

She'd been trying to keep busy ever since they'd been watching the horses early this morning. Learning to shoot a handgun, for one thing. It turned out she was a good shot. But the feeling of a handgun was totally different than a shotgun.

Afterward she'd worked with Sam to find hiding places in every room for a loaded weapon where Mikey couldn't reach. And now she sat on her bed making decorations out of materials she'd found in the attic for tomorrow's birthday party.

Sam had spent most of his day working with his brothers on perimeter safety for the house. And as the day wore on, his expression and his attitude seemed more and more concerned. Even though he'd said very little, she could tell. He prowled the rooms in a sort of harsh silence, most unlike his usual congenial attitude.

Grace was torn. If this place really had become that dangerous, she wanted to take Mikey and leave the area. Run again to somewhere else where the baby would be safer. Anywhere else.

On the other hand she'd started to fall in love with the ranch and the people on it. If she had only herself to consider, she would stay and wait for Jose to show up. In fact, she would be quite happy to end her running and take a stand right here on the ranch with Sam.

Maybe that idea would be something to consider. Hiding the baby somewhere else, with someone she could trust, so she and Sam could lead Jose off in another direction—hopefully to capture.

But could she leave Mikey? Not knowing how he was doing? Not watching him grow and making sure he was truly safe and happy?

A fist of cold fear gripped her heart at the thought. What could she stand to give up for the safety of her child?

Everything.

But the idea would take a lot more thought. She'd need to talk it over with Sam.

Coming out of her deep introspection to check on her napping baby on the blanket beside her, she noticed the dusk beginning to crawl in through the windows. Night was always the hardest time. Ever since Jose had taught her to fear silent shadows. To fret over every whisper of noise in the dark.

Sam's attentions had gone a long way toward changing her attitude about nighttime. But tonight she felt the shiver of fear clear down to the marrow of her bones.

She wanted the night to be over, despite still hoping for a repeat performance of last night in bed with Sam.

A faint rustling noise came from somewhere outside the room. It could be coming from anywhere. The sound seemed to her as if someone were sneaking across wood floors in their stocking feet. The hair on her arms stood on end.

"Hey, there you are." Sam opened the bedroom door and flipped on lights. "Everything okay?"

Mikey awoke at the noise and light and managed to sit up all by himself. "Mooh." He waved his hands, opening and closing the fingers.

"What's he want?" Sam stepped closer.

"His dinner, I think." Grace waited until her heartbeat slowed and then slipped off the bed. "I'll go down and fix him something."

"Let me." Sam picked up the baby and waited for her to stand.

"That would be nice. It'll give me time to put up some of these party decorations in the front room." She grabbed an armful of the brightly colored balls and the Happy Birthday sign she'd made.

She followed Sam and the baby out the door and down the stairs. "Have your brothers left?"

"Yes, ma'am. Travis and I worked most of the afternoon setting booby traps on the windows. And we rigged up a few nasty tricks in spots around the backside of the house, too." Sam shifted Mikey in his arms. "While Gage was here, he measured and checked the electrical circuits for the installation of an alarm system for the doors. He thinks the manufacturer can overnight a new system by tomorrow."

"That'll make me feel safer." But not as safe as having Jose back in jail would make her feel. "Sam, can we talk later tonight? I have an idea and I'd like to run it by you."

"Sure. After Aunt June brings out the groceries and Mikey is down for the night. Okay?"

"That's fine. Do you think June will get here quickly? It's getting dark."

"In the next half hour or so. She has to return Jenna to the ranch after watching her for Travis this afternoon. She'll be stopping at Travis's place first."

That sounded good. The sooner they could lock up the house for the night and barricade themselves inside, the better Grace would like it.

In the meantime she very much needed to ease the tension in her shoulders and speak in low, clear tones so the baby wouldn't notice her fears. Kids picked up on those things.

Grace stood on a small stepstool, finishing off her arrangement of decorations on the enormous wood and stone fireplace mantel in the front room. As she worked, she'd been listening to bits and pieces of Sam's voice while he jabbered to Mikey and fed him dinner in the kitchen.

Earlier this afternoon Sam had pulled all the drapes and closed the downstairs shutters. She couldn't see out, but then no one could see in.

Still, she knew the last fading tendrils of sunset must be on the western horizon. She was feeling antsy and her nerves were edgy. Every little noise in the house sent her heart racing.

She sure wished June would hurry up. To keep herself from collapsing with the stress, Grace began to hum. Starting with the "Happy Birthday" song.

Just as she finished tacking down the last nail to hold

up the large sign she'd made, she heard a soft knocking at the front door. At last.

Jumping down, she raced to the door and threw back the locks. "About time you arrived, June," she said as she wrenched the door wide open.

But it wasn't Sam's sweet-faced aunt on the other side. Instead two dark men stood on the threshold; both of them holding big, black pistols—aimed in her direction!

She started to slam the door in their faces, but they'd already barged inside. The bigger of the two grabbed her from behind and closed his big palm over her mouth.

"Silencio," he whispered in her ear.

The guy's hand stank of sweat and horses. On his breath, the smell of coffee and peppers. And the whole obnoxious odor seemed mixed with the stench of horse manure. Her stomach rolled.

"Where is *el niño de Serrano?*" The other gunman hissed his question in broken English mixed with Spanish.

She started to whine and squirm, trying to break free. Sam had hidden a gun behind a vase on the mantel. If only she could reach it, then these two goons wouldn't act so tough. But the guy holding her tightened his grip and the man that had spoken shoved his gun in her nose—hard enough to make her see stars.

"No noise. No trouble. Or I shoot. I shoot baby."

Oh, dear Lord. Mikey. Her heart pounded and she began to shake, the tremors coming from somewhere deep in her gut. But she wasn't ready to let fear overtake her senses. She needed to remain calm. And wait for her chance.

She hadn't really believed Sam when he'd said they needed to be more careful. That Serrano must be closing in. It had seemed impossible. But she would never doubt him again. If they both lived through this night.

The man with the gun in her face whispered to his companion in Spanish. "You check upstairs for the baby. Take the woman. And be careful not to let her call out. I will search downstairs. The lawman will be close by. Watch for him. He has to die."

Sam rose from his chair to pick up their dirty dishes. Baby Mikey had fallen sound asleep in the middle of his supper. Little guy must be tuckered out from all the fresh air today.

As Sam turned to the sink, he heard a strange noise. Not the same sounds of Grace working in the front room that he'd been hearing. He'd grown used to those over the past half hour. This sounded more like someone coming through the front door. At first he thought his aunt June must've arrived. But an instant later he realized that couldn't be true. He hadn't heard any vehicles driving up. And the rumbling sound June's old truck made was unmistakable.

Never hesitating, Sam gently picked up Mikey and a handful of dish towels. Finding a good spot on the floor behind a sack of flour in the pantry closet, he made a nest of towels for the baby. Laying Mikey in the center of the nest without disturbing him, he closed the door and prayed the boy wouldn't wake up or cry out in his sleep.

Grabbing his forty-five from a canister on the counter, Sam flipped off the lights and waited a second for his eyes to adjust. Then moving to stand behind the swinging kitchen door, his every sense went on alert. He listened carefully, heard footsteps on the stairs and knew someone was prowling around downstairs, too.

Damn. He'd been sure Serrano's men were close, but not this close. He should've taken more precautions. Or better yet, moved Mikey and Grace somewhere they would have greater protection.

Where was Grace? Sam was torn between staying in the kitchen to guard Mikey's hiding place and stealing down the hall to find her.

But he didn't have long to consider the options.

The sound of someone creeping along the hallway and coming closer was unmistakable. Only one set of footsteps. Good and bad news. Sam would have no trouble overpowering a lone gunman, but then he would probably have to deal with another man somewhere else in the house. Someone who might have Grace with him. Whatever Sam did next must be done quietly.

Then there it was. A faint squeak of the kitchen door hinge. The door inched open slightly and the shadow of a handgun preceded whoever it was into the room.

Sam held his breath, not making any sound, and waited. But the gunman was careful not to rush into anything. The weapon, a small-caliber German model, came through first. Next a hand appeared. A forearm.

And when a man's shoulder was just past the edge of the door, Sam shoved his weapon into his jeans' waistband and placed both hands against the wood. In a burst of power, he slammed the full force of his body against the back of the door in a surprise move.

The heavy old door made a good weapon as it hit its target. A thud and the sound of bone crunching. Then a groan. And the weapon went skidding across the waxed, pinewood floor.

Sam ripped open the door, stepped around it and reached for the man's injured arm.

The guy cursed in Spanish as Sam wrenched the obviously broken arm and drew him into the room, letting the door swing closed behind them. Sam was on him before the would-be gunman could catch his balance.

They tumbled across the floor and in seconds Sam had the guy pinned. Before he could yell out and warn his buddy, Sam closed the goon's big open mouth by shoving a fist into his teeth.

A sharp pain reverberated up Sam's arm when he connected, but the gunman thankfully fell silent. Sam shook him by the shoulders a couple of times and still got no response. Shaking out his aching hand, Sam stood and quickly ripped the cord from the window blinds to tie the assailant's hands and feet. Finally satisfied the guy was immobilized, he stuffed paper towels into his still-bleeding mouth to keep him quiet.

Grace. He had to locate her fast. Since he hadn't heard anything from her, Sam was positive another gunman must be holding her captive. And—what?

Searching for the baby? Had to be.

Sam left the lights off and slid out into the hallway with his forty-five back in hand. Starting up the stairs, he was careful not to step on any loose floorboards. He remembered the location of every single squeaky board from his teenage years.

At the top of the landing he stopped to listen. Noises were magnified in the darkness. He thought he heard a high-pitched whine, like a woman in distress. But he couldn't distinguish where the sounds were coming from. Until he saw a light seeping under the master bedroom door.

No other way to enter the bedroom but through that door. So Sam prepared himself in the hall, put his hand on the knob and burst into the room, hoping surprise might win half the battle.

But what he saw took him back for a second. A big burly man lay sprawled across the bed on top of Grace. Holding her in place with his body, the assailant kept her quiet with one beefy hand over her mouth.

Fury erupted in Sam like a sudden violent volcano. In that second all his training—all his vows to do everything by the book—every single thing that made him a lawman and a human being, went right out the window.

He'd killed before, but never in a blind rage such as this one. Closing in on the man, he felt a snarl twisting his features. As he grabbed the man by the shoulders, adrenaline surged and he roared out his anger.

As if the guy were a lightweight, Sam bodily lifted him off Grace and swung him around. A well-placed knee doubled the guy over and Sam's first punch rolled him onto the floor.

Still seeing red, Sam grabbed a handful of shirt to hold him steady then pounded his fist into the goon's face. Over and over. Every punch was payback for a day that Grace had suffered.

"Sam, stop!"

He wasn't sure how many times she'd said it before he finally lifted his head. With blurry eyes and foggy brain, he looked at her.

She stood over the two of them and appeared to be fine. "Don't hit him anymore, Sam. Where's Mikey?"

Mikey. He'd forgotten about him. "I left him sleeping on the floor of the pantry."

Grace turned and started for the stairs.

"Wait." Sam hauled himself off the belly of the downed goon. "Don't go near the other gunman. Give him a wide berth in the kitchen."

"Is he tied up?"

"Yeah. But maybe you'd better wait for me."

Without waiting or saying a word, Grace turned and dashed toward the stairs. Sam couldn't blame her. He was every bit as concerned about Mikey.

Still, he would have to deal with this unconscious beached whale before he could join Grace and Mikey in the kitchen. Looking down with disgust, Sam shook his head.

These two gunmen were Serrano's. That meant the head of the snake was still out there somewhere. Sam ground his teeth and found a length of cord to tie the bastard. As he did, the jerk seemed to be coming around. He mumbled something in Spanish. Sam ignored him.

But soon he would demand answers from one of these two. Wondering which of the gunmen would be the easiest to crack, Sam considered his options. He wanted Serrano. Now more than ever. How much would it take to make one of them give up his boss's whereabouts?

Sam had no compunction about torture. Not when Grace and Mikey's safety was at stake. But he didn't want to question these two in Grace's presence. Her psychological state was fragile at best. He couldn't put her through the ordeal.

But he needed help dragging both goons outside and finding somewhere private to interrogate them. He thought for a second about calling Gage.

Then the thing that had been sitting in the back of his mind finally broke through all the other thoughts. Where the hell was his aunt June? What had happened to her?

Instead of calling Gage, Sam pulled out his cell and called Sheriff McCord. The dispatcher at the Sheriff's Office said he was out on a call but would try to put Sam through.

When McCord answered, Sam began by giving his name.

Before Sam could add anything else, the sheriff interrupted. "I'm just coming up your porch stairs, son. What's your location in the house? Do I need backup? Your brothers are on the way."

"Upstairs, Sheriff. First door on the left. I have it handled. Where's my aunt June?"

McCord walked into the bedroom ten seconds later. "Your aunt is right outside, Chance. She arrived here and found the door open. When she noticed the downstairs was dark and there were two Bar-C horses saddled and tied out front next to your truck, she called Travis and he sent a copter to pick me up. I ordered her to hold her position outside. I'll let her in as soon as we're sure it's secure."

The sheriff helped Sam haul the chubby gunman to his feet. "You have another one of these creeps still in the house?" he asked.

"Downstairs in the kitchen. But he's subdued, too."

"Where's the woman and the baby?"

Mikey. And Grace.

As he took off down the stairs, Sam's world began to spin. It hit him how close he'd come to losing everything. Too damned close. Sam vowed this would be the last time he'd take any chances with either of their lives.

He had to find Serrano. The man had to go.

Chapter 19

Jose Serrano quit grinding his teeth and tried to breathe. Frustration gripped his gut as he looked around his hiding place. Staying here at a decent motel on the outskirts of San Angelo, Texas, he was no more than forty miles outside the town of Chance. But it was too far away from the action for him to be involved—or to give him the opportunity to see his own son.

Now he also had to face a small setback. He'd been secretly keeping a close eye on his two *empleados* Hector and Pedro. And had sent a trusted local man, a second cousin, to watch what they did. He didn't trust Hector. And it looked as if he'd been right to be skeptical.

Hector es un besugo! The fool hadn't taken time to make a good plan for the kidnapping and was apprehended as a consequence. The stupid one, Pedro, was off to jail along with his compadre.

Fortunately for them they could not tell the authorities a thing concerning his whereabouts. They hadn't known Jose had entered the United States a few days ago. Still, for their disobedience and impatience, they would find a nasty surprise awaiting them in prison. He had prison spies and people ready to do his bidding in both the Texas and federal prison systems.

He dismissed thoughts of the two morons with a toss of his chin. His more immediate goal was to have his son. He was eager to see the boy for the first time. Would his child look like his side of the family?

Miguel. The woman had named his son Miguel after her own grandfather. That was another treachery she would soon regret.

But the boy was young yet. His child could learn to accept a new name.

Calling his bodyguard in from the room next door, Jose ordered the preparation for their departure. Arrangements had been worked out yesterday with the cousin for Jose to steal into the town of Chance and hide out in the cousin's home. Plans made long before Hector and Pedro were captured earlier this evening.

The best way to win in this kind of situation was to outsmart—not overpower—the opposition. And Jose was sure he could do just that. He knew every detail of Sam Chance's background. And by now he had enough information on the man to predict his next move.

Chance would think he had time now that the original threat had been neutralized. He would believe the immediate danger was past. But still the lawman would act quickly to avoid any further surprise attacks. Jose could bet that the man's next act would be to move the quarries quickly. Away from the Bar-C. Maybe even out of Texas.

But not tonight. Tomorrow night.

Chance wouldn't count on the fact that Jose was already in the immediate area and ready to strike again. His guard would be lowered—enough for Jose to take advantage. Tomorrow.

Almost smiling at his tactical superiority, Jose gave another fleeting thought to an alternate plan for holding his position until after the quarries ran again. He was nearly certain he knew where Grace would want to go next. And positive that he understood Chance well enough to be waiting for them when they arrived there. Back in Los Angeles.

And in a few ways an ambush in Los Angeles would be the smarter move for Jose to make. He had a lot of contacts and an entire platoon of his own army living and working in the City of Angels. Clearly he would have the tactical advantage there, even though he had already ordered the execution of his currently useless federal contact. That man was no longer of value. He'd become a liability. Jose had many others who could take his place.

But he didn't want to wait. Jose wanted to see his son now. It would also be best if he didn't travel throughout the U.S., even in secret, when he was being hunted by the FBI and the federal Marshals.

No, his mother awaited her grandson in Mexico, and that was where Jose and his son would be. By the day after tomorrow.

The plans had been formulated and were already being implemented. And acting quickly was definitely **the smarter move when it came to Grace. A surprise** attack again the next day would be unexpected and should yield the easiest and best results.

He wanted his son. Now. And Jose Serrano always got what he wanted.

Sometime in the dead of night, Grace opened her eyes and blinked at the shadows cast by the nightlight burning in Sam's room. She turned her head on the pillow and looked straight into Sam's cool blue eyes looking back at her.

"How long have you been awake?" she whispered. "Have you gotten any sleep at all?"

After the sheriff, Sam's brothers, aunt and a variety of other ranch hands all left around midnight, they'd stationed a couple of hands outside the doors to keep watch for another attack. But Sam had still seemed edgy when he put Mikey down for the night and insisted she get some rest.

"Caught a couple hours' sleep," he told her. "You need your rest. I don't need much."

Maybe not, but the wrinkled creases at the sides of his eyes had deepened in the past few hours. He looked drawn and exhausted. She wanted to touch his face and smooth the stress away.

They needed to talk.

Instead Sam was the one to reach out to her. He gently pushed aside a strand of hair so he could lean in and tenderly place his lips against hers.

But the kiss suddenly turned hungry—greedy. The buzzing flurry in her chest instantly burst like a volcano of molten sensations going off. Every inch of her body burned with wanting, ached with longing for his caress.

Her hands went to his hair while his tongue slid inside her mouth. Sweet heaven. Hot agony.

She molded herself to him. Their legs aligned and his hard arousal settled against her soft belly.

Doing anything like this was foolish. They should talk. Or sleep. Despite her current need for rest and whatever came next for them, Sam would soon be going back to his job. Their whole future relationship was only something she'd created in her mind.

But as he touched her, as he kissed her as if he would never have enough, she couldn't help it. Her entire being centered on the *now*. She fell into the dream wide awake and forgot all about her reservations.

Already wet and wanting, she slithered out of her panties without breaking the kiss. As if they had choreographed their moves, he eased over her, still without breaking the kiss, and slipped quietly into her welcoming body.

Ah. The feel of him deep within her again was like coming home. She didn't have experience with any other lover but Jose. And that didn't count in her mind. But whatever she and Sam had together, however long it would last, it couldn't be wrong. She'd never felt so right in her entire life.

Leaning up on his elbows, he captured the sides of her head with his hands and gazed into her eyes. "I need you too much." His raw whisper sent waves of dizzying sensations to every tingling nerve. "I can't help myself. I won't let you rest or talk. I want you to distraction."

He began moving then. Slowly at first. And with each exquisite glide, she lost a little bit of her mind. Writhing under him, she moaned. Called out his name. Begging him to hurry the pace, she felt feverish and impatient.

But Sam never varied the tempo. His patience was maddening. Wrapping her legs around his thighs, she glued their sweaty bodies together and pushed her hips against his in wanton, fierce moves.

At last, when she'd been driven nearly crazy trying to reach that elusive something, the dam finally broke on his control. He cursed, plunged deeper and set a rhythm as wild as a hurricane. She met him stroke for stroke. Dug her fingernails into his shoulders and let herself go to wave after wave of shattering convulsions.

Peaking again and again, she shouted out in accompaniment to his gasping, roaring climax. Afterward she lay there holding him close and sobbing from the loss of breath and the strong emotions lingering in her heart. The exhilaration. The sense of being stripped to the essence of her soul.

But along with all that, also came the terrible, hollow and foreboding sense of coming loss.

"Are you okay? I didn't hurt you, did I?" Sam rolled over and lay on his back next to Grace.

She was still crying. More softly now. The sounds something like a whimper. Heartbreaking.

Grace shook her head and sniffed. "You could never hurt me, Sam. You're a protector. A man born to save the weak."

"You are hardly weak, Gracie." He'd never met a woman with so much strength of spirit.

All of sudden what he'd done hit him smack in the face. "Are you crying because I forgot to use protection? I swear, if that causes…if you are…" He couldn't figure out the best way to put this.

If she became pregnant with his child, he would be thrilled. But how could he tell her that? He had come to love Mikey as his own. Though that didn't mean he wouldn't love a baby brother or sister every bit as much.

How could he just assume she would want another baby? Or a future with him, for that matter?

Still, Grace's state of mind continued to be edgy. He could see it in a thousand little ways. And obviously, having a drug lord coming after you was not the very best time to start a new family.

A new family. Was that what he really wanted?

"Please don't worry, Sam," she said softly. "It's not the right time of month. If anything like that were to happen—well, we'd have to decide where to go from there. But this isn't a good time to be making plans that don't include Jose Serrano."

She smiled when she said it, and Sam knew it was her way of diffusing the conversation. But she was right. First Serrano. Then, whatever the future held.

Sitting up against the headboard, she pulled the sheet up under her arms. "Since we're up anyway, is this a good time to talk? I've had an idea about how we can deal with Jose."

So had he. But Sam was afraid she wasn't going to like his idea. He could easily imagine that the concept of putting her and Mikey back in WITSEC and then leaving them so he could go after Serrano in Mexico would not settle well. She was too overconfident in her own powers to protect herself and her child.

"Uh…okay." He scooted back against the headboard beside her and waited for her to go first.

"Well…"

Now he knew *he* wasn't going to like the sound of her idea, either. Setting his jaw and vowing to say nothing until she was finished, he crossed his arms over his chest and gave her room to hang herself.

"Sam, you know Jose has to be stopped. I will never

have another moment's rest until he's either back in jail or dead."

So far, they were in perfect agreement.

"And you also know, maybe better than I do, the difficulties of getting to him in Mexico."

He knew. He also knew it could be done. And he was the best man to capture the bastard. But only if she and Mikey were perfectly safe in the meantime.

"Well…" she began, sounding as if she was about to drop a bombshell on the room.

Here it came. This was bound to be good.

"What would you think of the idea of finding somewhere absolutely safe to leave Mikey. Somewhere Jose would never consider looking?"

"Just Mikey?"

"Yeah, I agree. It'll be hard for me to leave the baby behind with anybody. He's so little and there's not a lot of people I would trust with my son's life. But I've been thinking. What if we ask your brother Travis and your aunt June to take him? I would trust both of them with my life. Mikey's, too, in case of emergency. Which this is."

"Uh…"

"Think about it for a moment." She interrupted his train of thought and went on without stopping to listen to his objections. And he had plenty of objections.

"You and I could make a big show of leaving town with the baby. We could let the word get out that we're going to L.A. so the baby and I can be placed back into the Security Program. Everyone should buy that. Even Jose. It's logical."

Grace stopped to take a short breath and then plowed on. "Secretly we could leave Mikey with June. Just in case we were to be ambushed in the airport on the way to California."

"Actually," she added. "I think the baby might be a little safer on the Bar-C. But maybe June wouldn't mind moving out to Travis's until Jose is back in prison. It shouldn't take too long. Maybe a couple of months at most. You could ask her."

"Well, I don't know…"

"Wait until I finish, please. See, there's more to my plan."

Oh, so now she had a full-fledged plan. Obviously she'd given the idea a lot of thought. He shut his mouth and gave her more rope.

"This is the tricky part. So don't say anything until I'm completely finished."

He couldn't get a word in even if he wanted to. But this ought to be one hell of an idea.

"My idea is for me to lure Jose out of Mexico—using Mikey as bait. I know Jose. He will move heaven and earth to put his hands on his son. He's so arrogant. He'll think he can outsmart us and find a way of stealing the baby and taking him into Mexico. And probably killing me."

Sam looked down between them and discovered he'd covered her hand with his own. Already protecting. Already wanting to keep her from harm.

"I can send him a message," she went on. "That I've had a change of heart and I want my son to get to know his father. Jose is such an egotistical maniac that he would eat that up. And in the meantime, you and the FBI can be waiting to ambush him."

She heaved a deep sigh. "I'm so tired of being on the defensive where Jose is concerned. Hiding. Scared of every noise. It's time I became a little proactive."

Sam knew from the textbooks that a Stockholm syndrome patient taking back a sense of their own destiny was a good thing. A major breakthrough point in their recovery.

So he was glad she'd come up with a plan to eliminate Jose from her world instead of the other way around. And really glad she didn't want to keep on running for the rest of her life. He didn't like the idea of Grace contacting Serrano, however. Didn't like it at all.

Though he had to admit that maybe the idea of surreptitiously splitting her and Mikey up was the best thought she'd had. Serrano would never expect Grace to leave her baby with anyone else. And the drug lord wouldn't consider looking for the child in a place where he'd already been found, either.

"So, what do you think?" She sounded hesitant. Worried that he would say no.

And he should say no. Hell no. It was too dangerous for her. And he damned sure didn't want to be separated from Mikey. Not for a minute.

Surprised, he realized that he, too, trusted Travis and June with the baby's life. Something he wouldn't have considered only a few short weeks ago. Back then he barely trusted himself. Now family had become his backup?

He'd changed a lot over his time with Grace.

"Let me make a few phone calls." That wasn't what he'd wanted to say. "If we do things your way, it will have to be fast. We can't stay in this house another night. Serrano will have more henchmen heading this way fast if he thinks we're not running."

"I hate to leave here," she said quietly.

Yeah, he did, too. Amazing. He'd been in such a danged big rush to get out of this place as a kid.

"But I'm glad you think my plan has a chance." She was sounding unsure of herself again.

"You're positive you can stand leaving Mikey with June and Travis?"

She nodded. But Sam noticed she was much less enthusiastic when it came down to reality.

"Then let's get a move on. We have lots to do to put your ideas in motion today."

And he had even more to do if he was going to make two sets of plans. But he had to be sure she would be safe in L.A. He couldn't take any chances with her life.

Sam didn't trust Serrano to behave like she expected him to. In fact, he knew the bastard would pull something totally unexpected.

But Sam vowed he would be prepared—for absolutely anything the son-of-a-bitch could throw at them.

Chapter 20

"Turn around and check on the baby." Sam kept his hands on the wheel and didn't look toward her to speak. "I want it to appear as though we're going to visit June before we head out of town to the airport. Nothing out of the ordinary. It's got to look like we aren't worried about being followed now that Serrano's men have been captured."

Grace's jangled nerves wouldn't allow her to utter a word. But she swiveled in her seat and pretended to fiddle with Mikey's seat belt. Only it wasn't Mikey in the car seat. It was a large baby doll that Sam had rescued from the attic. It wasn't even Mikey's real car seat but an ancient one that Travis had kept from Jenna's baby years.

"I'm not sure I can go through with this," she told Sam as she righted herself again in the seat.

"What? Leaving the baby with Travis and June? That was your idea, remember."

She remembered. She'd been kicking herself for making the suggestion all day long. But being separated from her baby wasn't her biggest worry right now.

"No, it's not that. I trust your brother and your aunt to keep him safe. But I'm not sure I can be a good enough actress to fool anyone with our charade. All the way through the airport and right up to screening? The idea scares me to death."

"You'll do fine. Try to remember how to pretend the way you did in childhood."

Grace wasn't sure she did anything remotely like pretending when she was a kid. Every time she tried to think back to those times, her parents came to mind. And that immediately brought up the vision of her mother and father—fighting to get out of their office after the explosion.

Dear Lord, what she had done was horrible. She'd blithely betrayed her loved ones. Without giving it much thought. She had let her anger at them, anger cleverly provoked by Jose, give him the answer to a way in. A way for the *devil* to destroy everything her family held dear.

Though she hadn't known her parents would be at the office when it went up in flames, she was still to blame for their deaths. The idea of going back to L.A. to face her memories squarely terrified her.

But she couldn't let Sam know. This was the best idea anyone had for capturing Jose. And she was definitely the only one who could coax him out of hiding. Pretending to dangle his child in front of him like a rabbit in a trap waiting for the wolf would do the trick.

Her real child was safe now. And if it meant she had

to die to keep him that way and end the threat from Jose for good, so be it. She'd been staying alive for Mikey. And now for Sam.

Sneaking a glance at his profile, she made a promise to herself. Sam could not be hurt during this charade. She knew he thought he was going to capture Jose without her. She could feel it in his responses to his family and to the baby. He didn't think he was coming back from this trip.

But it was she that might not be coming back. Sam had to live. He would raise her baby as though Mikey was his own. Grace would gladly sacrifice her life for her child's, but only if she felt assured her baby would be raised with love. Sam would do that. Sam would save her child and give him the kind of life she wanted him to have.

She would find a way to kill the *devil*. Somehow. This wasn't a plan for revenge. It was pure, cold logic. As powerful as Jose was, he would never stop until she was dead and he had Mikey. But she vowed he would never have her son. Or the man she loved.

"We're almost to June's." Sam drove slowly down the town's side streets. "Great timing. It's dusk. Anyone watching will believe we're just dropping by for supper before leaving town."

He'd asked June to spread the word around town today that they would be flying out from the San Angelo airport with the baby tonight. On their way to L.A. Grace wasn't so positive Jose would hear the news. After all, he was still in Mexico and his men here had been captured last night.

But Sam seemed convinced Jose would know. Sam was no doubt right. The *devil* had an army of spies stationed in several countries. It wouldn't be much of a trick for him to have more men around the town of Chance.

"Will you be the one to take the fake Mikey out of his car seat? Please? I don't think I can do a credible job of it."

Sam gave her a reassuring smile. "Sure. Don't look so worried. Everything is going to be fine. You trust me, don't you?"

"Of course."

"Then don't give it a lot of thought. I'll handle things. This was your idea, but I'll help you get through the details. Okay?"

It was okay for now. But somehow on their way to L.A. she would have to get a hold on her nerves and start playing her part. She had no intention of Sam being caught between her and Jose when it came right down to it. So she would have to stay a step ahead.

As Sam pulled up in front of June's house and everything looked quiet and peaceful, Grace calmed down. This was the easy part. Nothing could go wrong here.

Sam held the doll, covered over with a baby blanket, between his forearm and chest. While Grace pranced up the stoop ahead of him, carrying a large diaper bag. The bag was large enough for the fake Mikey to slide inside when going through airport screening.

They were running later than he'd planned. Dusk had become deep shadows and soon complete darkness would descend. And June's interior lights were already giving off a warm glow. He didn't care for traveling across the Texas plains at nighttime. Too easy to be ambushed somewhere along the way.

If Serrano got wind Grace was running with Mikey again, he wouldn't hesitate to send more henchmen to intercept them. Sam decided on a quick change of plans. He would take Sheriff McCord up on his offer of an escort from Chance to the San Angelo airport. Calling the sheriff from his aunt's house would be no trick and it shouldn't take long to round up a cruiser and a couple of deputies to accompany them at least as far as the interstate.

Grace knocked on the always-unlocked front door. And upon hearing a distant "Come in," she turned the knob and walked inside. The moment she was out of sight, Sam knew something was wrong.

Never in his memory could he remember his aunt June inviting people inside without meeting them at the door. Picking up his pace, he ran to the front stoop and reached for the doorknob.

Before he could push open the door, out of the shadows and bushes came two men who jumped him. One pulled the doll from his hold while the other put a gun to his temple.

"Inside, gringo. Senor Serrano wishes to talk." The man with the gun ripped his arm around and held him fast as they marched in step into the house.

Serrano was here and not in Mexico? If it wasn't for Grace and June, Sam would be grateful to the drug lord for making his job easier. Serrano didn't know it yet, but he would not be leaving Chance a free man. He had just made his first big mistake.

But before he could take down Serrano, Sam needed to make sure Grace and June lived through the coming showdown.

The goon at his side shoved Sam into the kitchen. What he saw could've unnerved him. Instead he set his jaw and cleared his mind.

Serrano had June seated and tied up in a high-backed

chair. But she looked unharmed. On the other hand, Grace was being manhandled by another goon while Serrano held her at gunpoint. A big S.O.B., the man standing over Grace was feeling her up.

Sam's fury hit hard and fast, but he bit back his anger. "I should've known you were bound to be unsophisticated and uncool, Serrano. Of course you'd need a goon and a gun in order to manipulate a woman into doing what you want."

"Silencio!" The man beside Sam hit him in the side of the head with the butt of his gun.

Briefly Sam lost consciousness as he staggered to one knee. But he came around fast enough to focus on the man in charge. Serrano laughed at the sight of Sam on his knees, but he walked toward Grace.

Slapping her hard across the face, the drug lord spit out the words. "You have kept my child from me, whore. For too long. It is now over. I will have my son. And you will have nothing. Not even another sunrise."

Everyone stopped in their places and stared at the man in charge who was waving a thirty-eight handgun around the room. "Alfredo, take the boy to the 4x4 out back. Strap him in the child's carrier in the backseat and stay with him until I join you. Nothing is to happen to that baby. You understand? Nothing."

The goon holding fake Mikey mumbled his acceptance of his boss's order and turned around to leave by the front of the house. Sam wondered how long it would take for the idiot henchman to figure out they'd been had and report back to his boss.

Sam needed just enough time to overpower the other two and lay his hands on Serrano.

But Serrano seemed to sense Sam's plans. "Rodriguez, take the lawman in the other room and hog-tie him on the floor. Make sure you pat him down for weapons and then tie him good, like you would a rabid animal."

Grace's eyes widened and Sam tried to throw her a reassuring glance as the goon beside him hauled him to his feet. But Serrano was already standing between them with the thirty-eight and a wide-bladed knife in his hands while Sam was unceremoniously dragged into the living room.

Hang in there, darlin'. Do not give up. We'll beat the bastard in the end.

Grace wanted to scream. To yell at Jose and tell him to let Sam go. But so far she had maintained her composure. And she wouldn't give him the satisfaction of hearing her plead now.

They weren't dead yet. Jose didn't even know about Mikey yet. She and Sam might have a chance. But she needed to keep her head and not do anything stupid. Nearing hysteria already, Grace ignored her stinging cheek. And tried not to think of how her shoulders ached from being held with her arms behind her back.

Jose came closer. "You are still beautiful, my Bella. Becoming a mother has only added to your charms. I wish I had the time to show you what you still do to me."

He tenderly laid the steel blade of the knife against the side of her nose. "And I should also show you how Jose Serrano treats traitors. Though it would be a shame to cut into that beautiful face."

She held her breath and kept her mouth shut, waiting for the first nick. She wouldn't put it past Jose to want to torture her for turning him in and taking her son.

"Sadly," Jose added, "we do not have time for either one. Another ten minutes and it'll be dark enough for us to leave. Unfortunately for you, this sunset will be your last."

He turned to the big goon who was holding her fast and spoke to him in Spanish. "Tie the woman and leave her in the other room with her paramour. When you are finished, take the old lady out to the 4x4. She will make a good *abuela* for the baby until we reach my mother's casa."

Grace wondered if she and Sam would be shot and left here at June's. Neighbors were close by. Someone would hear the gunshots. Should she mention that fact to Jose? She didn't wish to take any chances of egging him into a rage.

Turned out, she didn't need to say a word.

Once Jose was convinced her ropes were secure, he glanced longingly at the front door. "I am going out to the 4x4 to meet my son while we get the old lady settled."

He pointed the tip of his huge knife at Sam and then turned it back to her. "You two have become a liability. I'd like to end it right here and make things simpler all around. But it would be best if you are seen leaving town. The sheriff no doubt will be looking out for your truck to head to the airport tonight. We shall accommodate him.

"Besides, there's a lot of empty land between here and Mexico," he added needlessly. "And it'll take the law a long while to find and identify the bodies out in that wasteland. Plenty of time for me and my son to arrive safely at home."

With that he turned his back on them and waited for his huge henchman to drag June, kicking and moaning, out the front door ahead of him. Then Jose calmly followed them outside and shut the door.

Sam lifted his head against his ropes. "Are we alone in the house?"

"Are you all right? He didn't hurt you, did he?"

"We don't have much time, Grace. Any minute Serrano will discover he's been had and be back here ready to take off our heads. Can you scoot closer?"

Her ropes were looser than Sam's, and her hands tied in front. But she couldn't break the ties on either her hands or feet. Still, she had the leverage to inch her bottom along the carpet in Sam's direction.

"Good girl. That's far enough. Now, can you manage to put your fingers on the tip of my boot?"

She did as he asked. Not sure what came next.

"Press down on the top of the scroll work there. You don't need to press too hard. Just..."

Suddenly a blade shot out of the tip of his boot, nicking her on the index finger. She kept the cry of pain bottled up and breathed deep.

"Quick, position your hands over the blade and let me rock my toe against the ropes. It should only take a moment to—" The ropes broke with a whoosh of air. "That a girl. Good work."

Sam had been right. Three or four good swipes with his sharp blade and her hands were free.

"What now?" she asked as she untied her feet. She was getting more frantic by the moment.

"No time for mine. Get the Glock out of the box on June's mantel."

"Glock?" He'd hidden a gun at June's?

"Hurry."

She took the gun in hand and checked to be sure it was loaded. "What now?"

"Dial 1 on that phone on the desk. It's the sheriff."

While making the call, she inched back toward Sam.

She would much rather he took charge of the gun. Five more minutes and she would have him free of the ropes.

Just as the sheriff's dispatcher answered, the door burst open.

"*Puta!* What have you done with my son?" Jose stood in the doorway, the anger shooting off of him like fireworks.

He drew the big, ugly knife out of his belt and started toward her.

"Stay back," she warned as she dropped the phone. "This gun is loaded, Jose. I swear I'll use it."

Snarling at her, he ignored her words and took another menacing step. "Where is the boy? You know what I can do with a knife, Bella. It won't be pretty."

Her hands were shaking, but she planted her feet and held the gun in both hands the way Sam had trained her. "Stop! I mean it."

Jose did stop for a second, but then he turned his attentions on Sam. "Tell me what I want to know, whore. Or we will see how many stab wounds this Anglo bastard can stand before he dies."

"Leave him alone!" She lost focus for one second as her hands shook harder and her eyes hazed over.

"Don't listen to him, Grace. Hold your position." Sam couldn't look up to see either Jose or her because of the way he was tied. But his words were solid and encouraging.

"Shut up, gringo." Jose stood before Sam and raised the knife above his head. "She doesn't have the courage to shoot a man. But she will tell me what I want to know or she will see how you suffer."

"Stop," she said one more time. "Don't."

"You make me sick," Jose said. "No answers? Fine. Watch your lover die."

The blade began a downward arch, heading for Sam's broad back.

Grace heard the repeated sounds of gunfire. Blast after blast. Close by. And she smelled the sulfur stench of gunsmoke. But it took a few seconds for her to realize that the sounds and smells had come from the gun in her hand.

Jose stopped with his arm in midair. He turned and took a step in her direction, then he sank to his knees and finally collapsed in a heap on the floor.

"Grace! Grace!" Sam's voice was frantic but she could barely hear what he was saying. "Watch out for Serrano's men. Take your position again."

She let the gun drop from her fingers. It was done. Jose Serrano would never again be a threat to Mikey.

Chapter 21

Struggling against his bonds, Sam continued calling Grace's name. But no answer came.

Visions of her haunted his mind, devastated and trembling, waiting for Serrano's men to end it all. She was so close to freedom. So close to finding a permanent escape from the man who'd hounded her days and dreams. Sam couldn't stand the thought of her dying just at the climax of her troubles.

He'd nearly managed to free his right hand when he heard footsteps coming up the front stoop and men's voices shouting in Spanish. No. Not now.

"Grace!" His heart pounded out a staccato beat.

Then he heard someone say in perfect Texas lingo, "Is he dead? Confiscate the gun. There on the floor." The voice was familiar.

"Grace, say something! Where are you?" He needed to hear her voice.

But the next thing he felt was a pair of rough hands as they worked to free him from his ropes. "She's okay, Chance. A little shell-shocked. But uninjured."

Raising his head, Sam looked up into the weathered face of Sheriff McCord. He had never been so glad to see the man in his entire life.

The sheriff did away with the ropes and then headed back out the front door to finish rounding up Serrano's men. It took Sam a few seconds to get the feeling back in his hands and feet once he was free. But the instant he could stand, he was up and searching for Grace. He found her sitting in the kitchen with one of the town's volunteer firemen taking her pulse and blood pressure.

Her chin was lowered as she stared at her hands. He couldn't ever remember seeing her look quite this dejected.

Uh-oh. Had Jose's death tipped her previous unstable mental state over the edge?

"Grace." No response. "Gracie," he murmured in a softer tone.

That seemed to break through the fog. She finally looked up at him.

"Sam? You're okay. Thank God."

"I'm okay. How are you?"

The fireman answered the question for him. "Her pulse is a little high but the blood pressure readings are steady. Doesn't have a scratch on her. And except for that purple bruise just coming out on her cheek she seems fine."

Sam winced when he noticed the bruise. Damn that Serrano. Good thing the bastard was already dead.

"How's my aunt June?" he asked the fireman.

"Already checked her over. She looked great. Mad as a fire ant but physically in good shape. I live in the neighborhood and I know she's a tough old bird. No Mexican drug gang could stop June Chance for long."

Nodding and relieved, Sam turned to gaze at Grace but spoke to the fireman. "Can you give us a few minutes?"

"Sure." The man stood and patted Grace's shoulder. "The sheriff is going to need a statement from each of you. He wasn't happy to learn of the doll and your trick to lure Serrano. Thought the least you could've done was tell him the truth. Earlier tonight he'd been quietly circling the neighborhood, checking on y'all. Royally pissed him off when he heard gunshots."

Ignoring the guy's remarks, Sam pulled a chair beside Grace and sat. "Tell McCord we'll stay in here until he needs us. I don't want Grace to go back in the living room until the body is removed."

After the fireman was gone, Sam took her by the hand. "Talk to me, Gracie. What's going on with you?"

She didn't look at him, but spoke in a low voice. "Jose Serrano. He's really dead, Sam."

"Yeah, he's dead. But he's not my biggest worry at the moment. You are. Taking the life of another living being is not a simple thing. You can't just brush it off. It'll do a number on your conscience if you let it. And I don't want you to feel guilty about this. Serrano was a bad man. The worst of the worst. You saved the U.S. government a lot of trouble by ending it here."

At last she turned to look at him. "I'm not upset and I don't feel guilty. Not in the least. Can't say I feel like having a party, but I'm not sorry he's dead."

Pausing, she looked down at their joined hands and sighed. "I'm not sorry I was the one who killed Jose, either. He deserved to die, Sam. For what he did to my parents—to so many other parents and children over the years."

Sam put his arm around her shoulders, felt her trembling. She was putting up a good front. But she couldn't be as tough as she let on.

"I know the concept of justice, darlin'. Know it intimately. But, believe me, you're not meant to be the judge, jury and executioner. It isn't in you."

This time when she looked up, it was with a smile in her eyes. "I'm okay. Really. Jose will never be in our lives again. It's over. I want to see Mikey now."

Sam didn't like it. She shouldn't take something this big so nonchalantly. It was fine if she felt enormous relief in being freed from the fear. But not this too-too-casual attitude. Over the years he'd been forced to take several men's lives and had always felt remorse.

It made him wonder if her response was somehow connected to the Stockholm syndrome he felt sure she'd experienced when being held by Serrano. Just because her nemesis was dead did not mean all her problems were solved.

She needed help. More help than he could give her anymore.

"We'll see Mikey as soon as we talk to the sheriff," he told her. "And I won't let him keep us too long. What you did was in self-defense. That's all there is to it. You're the victim here. Not that bastard."

"I know." She was smiling now.

Sam's whole life and all his future dreams stopped dead in that one smile. He'd been building castles in the air with her and Mikey. Crazy of him. She would probably need years of therapy. Who was he to think he could help?

She'd made a tremendous difference in his life. He

no longer saw only his failures when he looked into the past. Her wisdom had given him a more rounded view. He now saw that he'd accomplished a few good things in his time. Helped to save more than a few good people.

He'd thought he could pay that forward by saving her life. By being the one who took out Serrano so she could live free.

But she'd handled that on her own. Now what could he do?

His first thought was to capture her in his arms and hide her away from her problems on the old homestead. In his bed. In his heart. The three of them, he wouldn't forget about Mikey, could be happy living on the Bar-C. He was sure of it.

But his second and third thoughts were more practical. He. Could. Not. Help. Her. Anymore. He needed to get that through his thick skull. Her problems went well beyond his areas of expertise.

Tomorrow he would call his boss—if he still had a job, that is. The Marshals and the FBI needed to be informed about this ambush. They might be willing to give Grace a reward for stopping Serrano.

The very least the FBI could do would be to let her see one of their specializing psychologists. Someone who deals with Grace's particular problem.

And what would he do while she got help somewhere else? The ache in the middle of his chest told the harsh truth. Give up his dreams. Let them go for good. And after that he'd better get back to work. After all, he could not bear to live on the ranch without Grace and Mikey.

"We need to leave tonight for L.A." Sam's voice broke through her thoughts.

"L.A.?" She thought perhaps she'd only dreamed that

he said it. "Jose has only been gone for thirty-six hours. What are you talking about?"

She'd been sitting here in the kitchen with Mikey playing on the floor, having happy fantasies centered around them living on the ranch for good. She and Sam and Mikey. Her baby would learn to ride and shoot and become a good honest man like his new daddy.

Instead Sam wanted them to go back to L.A.?

"Us." He waggled a finger between them. "Going back to L.A."

"Why?" The minute the word was out of her mouth, she could tell something was wrong. They must not be sharing the same dreams of the future.

There hadn't been much time to talk since the shooting. They'd spent all the day after speaking with the sheriff, looking at mug shots and retelling their stories. Things were crazy and confusing around the ranch and the town right now. The FBI had even flown in last night to interview them and pick up the body.

But through it all she'd felt sure they were in sync over where to go from here. She loved him. And she was positive he loved her in return. They would marry and live happily on the ranch.

Now the look in his eyes was hard. Unloving for the first time in weeks. The lawman was back. Had she been tricking her mind into believing something was true because she'd wanted it so much?

"I've had an interesting phone call. Seems my old boss at WITSEC has just been found dead in his car. An assassination is the way it looked. One bullet to the back of his head."

"Oh. But who…?"

"Serrano apparently."

"He's dead. How could he…? He *is* dead, isn't he, Sam?"

"He's definitely dead. But this was a hit Serrano ordered right before he came to Texas for Mikey."

"Why? Why would Jose order the death of your boss?"

She knew it was a stupid question. Jose liked death. He used it for everything. To pave the way. For payback. To convince someone he was right. To take care of someone who'd disagreed.

"Allegedly my boss was on Serrano's payroll. It turns out he was the bastard who gave Serrano the lead on your whereabouts. He also was the one who had my phone bugged with a GPS chip that I thought had been removed. And finally he gave Serrano my secure HR files. That's how the gang got the idea of coming to Chance to look for us."

Sam twisted and started pacing the floor. "Serrano paid the creep big bucks for help breaking him out of jail during his trial. I can't believe I never really knew the guy. Not in all the years I worked for him."

"How can the FBI know about this so soon? Who called you? Maybe the information is wrong."

Shaking his head, Sam stopped pacing and gazed at her. "It was the Special Agent in charge in L.A. who called. Their intel is solid. They've had a man undercover and embedded in Serrano's L.A. gang for six months, gathering evidence. They're closing the sting on the rest of the drug gang as we speak. Rounding up as many members as they can locate."

"But that's good. Why do we have to go to L.A. now?" She still wasn't ready to face her demons in L.A. And she and Sam still needed time and space alone to talk.

"The FBI lawyers want to depose you for the record. And they insist you see a psychologist. They don't want one of their star witnesses being accused of having PTSD."

"But that's idiotic. I'm not *crazy.* You know I don't have post-traumatic stress disorder. Tell them."

"Gracie…" He took her hand, sat beside her and stared into her eyes. "You may not have PTSD but I do think you would benefit from talking to a psychologist. Why not give it a try?"

She couldn't think of a good reason why not. In fact, she could barely think of anything while Sam's thumb made lazy circles on the palm of her hand.

"I…uh…" She searched Sam's eyes for some sense of what he felt.

Did he still want her and Mikey? Had their relationship been based on him keeping them safe and now that the danger was gone it was over? She wanted some sign. Some word or move that would tell her he would be sorry if they had to separate.

"I just don't want to leave the ranch," she finally managed. "I don't want to go back to California."

"It's time, Gracie. You have commitments. Your parents' estate needs you for final settlement, for one thing. And I understand your grandmother has been asking to see you. The FBI lawyers won't come to us, either, you know."

"But…" She didn't deserve anything from her parents' estate. And she couldn't bear to face her grandmother after what she'd done. In her opinion all those things were good reasons for her *not* going back.

Sam dropped her hand and stood. "It's time I go back to work, too. I'm needed at the WITSEC office in L.A.

to help straighten out the mess my boss left with his death."

There it was. The sign she'd been waiting for. But it was the one thing she'd dreaded to hear.

He was going back to work. Leaving the ranch. And he didn't seem ready to even discuss it.

"Do we have to leave so soon?" That wasn't what she'd wanted to say.

She wanted to say what was in her heart. To tell him she loved him and was desperate to make a life with him.

It didn't really matter whether they were here on the ranch or in L.A. Just as long as they were together.

"Afraid so. We have obligations, Gracie. And as much as I might like one more night in fantasy world with you, it's time to get back to reality."

Fantasy world? That's what he thought of their time together?

She could feel her heart tearing in two. This wasn't fair. He'd obviously been as happy with her as she was with him. But he was ready to see it end.

The one time when she'd found true happiness, and now she discovered the man she loved thought of their whole relationship as only a temporary dream?

Could her life get any more screwed up?

Chapter 22

Sam sat back in his chair and stared at the thick manila envelope sitting on his desk like it was a rattler poised to strike. A package from Grace?

It had been six long weeks since he'd seen Grace and Mikey. Six weeks of pure torture, knowing they were as close as a phone call but keeping his distance anyway.

He'd checked on them. By bribing the FBI to tell him what they knew. And he probably always would keep tabs.

But they didn't need him anymore. Grace made amends to her grandmother for not maintaining contact after her parents' funeral. In fact, she and Mikey were living with the older woman while Grace settled her parents' estate and went daily to see her psychologist.

Turned out Grace was a very rich woman. And getting better mentally if the psychologist's reports to the

Bureau were to be believed. Mikey, too, seemed to be thriving by all accounts. Loving the attention he'd been getting from his great-grandmother and the new friends in his day care.

But dang, Sam missed them both.

Last week he'd turned in his resignation and had begun training a replacement. He'd taken that final step because at last he'd figured out the truth. Simply being away from the Bar-C did not mean he would forget about Grace and Mikey. It didn't matter where he lived. He would always mourn the loss of the one woman he wanted above all others. Nothing he could do, no place he could go, would erase her and Mikey from his mind.

But she'd helped him see how much he had missed his roots. The ranch. His family. He belonged on the Bar-C and that's where he was most needed.

Today he'd been arguing with himself over whether to let her know he was going back to Texas. So far he'd checked on Grace and Mikey from afar in order to live up to a promise to her psychologist that he would give her enough time and space to find her own way back. Maybe the best thing now would be for him to contact her from the ranch. That way he wouldn't be tempted to beg her to come with him.

In all this time, all these days and hours, he had not heard one word from Grace until today. Not a phone call or an email. He'd hoped…

Looking down at the package addressed to him in her hand, Sam wondered if he had the nerve to open it. What if she was writing to tell him goodbye for good?

Deep down he knew it was over between them. And probably a complete cut, when he was leaving L.A. anyway, would be for the best.

But somehow he couldn't bring himself to actually

read the words. To see her saying that she was feeling well and starting a new life without him. Finding a new love. A new daddy for Mikey.

The damned envelope had been sitting there unopened for hours.

Stretching, Sam sat up. Time to be a man and take the bad news. It wouldn't change anything as far as he was concerned. But obviously it was important to Grace.

After using a knife to slit open the envelope, he dumped the contents on the desk. A letter and a small notebook.

He touched the notebook cover. Soft leather. It made him think of Grace on the ranch. Was this her journal?

Had she spent her days entering thoughts on these pages? He picked up the notebook and sniffed the cover. Yes, he could smell her scent. And she was giving it to him? As a goodbye gift?

Placing the notebook back on the desk, he picked up the letter. He needed to get the worst over quick.

But there were only a few lines written by hand on the paper. And none of them were what he'd expected.

Dearest Sam,
I am doing much better. Making peace with my mind monsters and guilt demons.

Mikey and I miss you very much. This week the psychologist suggested that I send you my daily journal. In it I wrote all my deepest thoughts, fears and hopes so I could truly be free. But now I know I won't be free until you read them, too.

I wish you the best of everything, Sam. You saved my life in more ways than one. I will never forget you.

With all my love, Grace.

* * *

Grace knelt in the dappled shade of an old oak tree. The scents of summer: the newly mown grass, the fragrant flowers and that special sunshiny smell of the breeze at this time of year, all gave her comfort. This was the last task on her list. The one thing she knew must be accomplished before she could move on with her life.

But it had taken every bit of her energy to force herself out of bed this morning. She'd been crying for two days straight. Ever since her last thread of hope disappeared. She waited by the phone, hour after lonely hour, praying to hear something from Sam after she'd sent her journal. Yet silence was all that met her tears.

Swiping the remnants of those tears from her eyes, she focused her attention instead on the large grave marker before her.

> **Dennis and Louisa Ramirez Randolph,**
> **loving parents of Isabella Grace Randolph.**
> **May they rest in God's embrace.**

The marker had turned out nicely. Her grandmother had been right about what it should say.

Now Grace had come to bid her goodbyes. She had been in Jose's clutches during her parents' funeral. But her grandmother had insisted the headstone should wait until she could make her choices. Grace had needed to be here on the day it was installed. Needed to shred this last remaining rope around her heart.

Her parents had been gone for nearly three years. And in all this time, she had not been able to drag herself to their gravesite. Not until today.

Sam's loving concern and six weeks of intensive therapy had made her see the truth. She'd finally accepted that their deaths were not her fault. Only one person deserved the blame. And Jose Serrano was already facing his maker for his sins.

"I wish things were different," she whispered to the wind. "I wish you could meet your grandson. Mikey is such a joy. You would love him as everyone else does."

Grace placed a bouquet of spring flowers at the base of the headstone. "And I wish you could've known Sam. He's such a good man."

The tears started again but she sniffed them back. "He would've been like the son you never had. Sam's the best, Mom and Dad. And even though he thinks he can't be with Mikey and me, I still…"

"You still what?" Sam's voice interrupted her solitary thoughts.

She swiveled around and glanced up, dumbfounded to see him standing there. Her voice suddenly fled as she gaped at him.

Surprisingly, he didn't pull her to her feet but knelt beside her. "Is it okay for me to be here?"

Swallowing past her dry throat, she nodded. "How long have you been standing there? And why are you here? How did you find me?"

"I've been here for about five minutes. Your grandmother told me where to find you. And as for why I'm here, that should be easy to explain, too. But…"

Her trembling must have been obvious because he inched closer and put his arm around her shoulders, giving her both strength and warmth at the same time.

"Tell me why. I need to hear it."

"You *deserve* to hear it, darlin'. You deserve to hear it every day for the rest of your life."

He cleared his throat. "I love you, Grace. I love you.

I love you." Pulling her closer, he placed a kiss against her temple and whispered in her ear. "I'm so sorry I didn't tell you before. But I don't want to live another day without telling you. Please say I'm not too late. That you still love me and forgive me for being such a jerk."

Her dry throat was gone, suddenly replaced by a huge lump. "You..." She swallowed hard. "If you read my journal, you know I still love you. I'll never stop."

"Oh, I read it all right. Maybe five times straight through—so far."

For some reason the idea of him reading her journal over and over made her smile. "It's not a bestseller. I think five times is plenty."

Sam took her by the shoulders, leaned in and kissed her on the lips. It was a kiss full of promise. Full of hope. And full of love.

The tears rolled down her cheeks as he broke the kiss and leaned back to gaze lovingly at her face.

"Why didn't I hear from you?" she managed to ask after a deep breath. "Why didn't you call?"

Sam flicked a tear from her cheek with his thumb. "I didn't call while you were in therapy because your psychologist asked me not to. He thought you should be free to work on you instead of worrying about us."

"But..."

"Yeah, I know. I should've gone with my gut and called anyway. I'm sorry."

"Then why didn't you call when you first received my journal?" He wasn't getting off the hook that easy.

Sam's expression turned sheepish. "It took me a whole day to get up the nerve to read it. I thought...you were trying to tell me goodbye."

She could certainly understand that. The two of them hadn't ever been the best communicators.

"Well, that's an excuse for one day. What about yesterday? After you did read it."

"I was busy."

"At work?" She couldn't understand. He seemed so eager to tell her he loved her but something else had kept him away for a full day?

Reaching into his jacket pocket, Sam pulled out a small blue velvet box. "Not at work. In fact, before you open this, I need to tell you something. I resigned."

She hadn't breathed since he'd produced the box, but she inhaled with those words and said, "You quit? What are you going to do?"

"I was planning on going back to the ranch. But now…" He hesitated and his words trailed off.

He opened the box and she stared down at the most beautiful emerald ring she had ever seen. "Will you and Mikey marry me, Grace? We'll live wherever you want to live. I'd be happy living on the moon if you two are there with me."

He slipped the ring on her finger. "Say yes."

Her eyes blurred as she stared up into the face of the man she loved more than life. "Yes. Yes. Yes! Mikey and I would love to marry you. And if we have a choice, we choose the ranch over the moon, please."

She threw her arms around his neck and kissed him again. This time she wanted to let him know how she felt. Sinking into him, she put all her dreams and hopes for their future into the kiss. But she couldn't get close enough. Their clothes kept getting in the way.

As he came up for air, Sam chuckled and said in a raspy tone, "Easy there. It's a little too wide-open here for that. We have lots of time. All the time in the world. Let's go find somewhere to be alone."

The sun burst through the leaves as he helped her to her feet. Yes, they had lots of time. A whole lifetime full of happy tomorrows. She couldn't wait.

Epilogue

Sam stood in the yard behind his old family homestead watching as his new bride picked up their son and danced him around to the two-step music.

He couldn't believe his luck. Grace was the most gorgeous bride he had ever seen. She'd let her hair grow out to its natural dark chestnut color. It bounced seductively against the silver satin material on her shoulders while she whirled and twirled.

The two of them were working hard on learning to communicate with each other. As he'd suspected, they'd found they had the same values and the same dreams for the future. And now that they were almost finishing each other's sentences, he figured they'd be a good fit for the next sixty years or so.

And Mikey. He was so proud of his boy, he could barely contain his love. Mikey was walking, really running most of the time, and talking up a blue storm.

Jenna had promised to teach her little cousin how to ride. And Mikey's mama wanted him to have shooting lessons just as soon as he was ready.

Sam didn't care what Mikey learned. As long as he was doing whatever made him happy.

Grace handed the baby over to Travis and glided over to stand beside him. "Hello, husband. What's on your mind?"

He swung her off her feet and twirled her around like she'd done for Mikey. "Just you, darlin'. Just you. You look like the barn cat who'd swallowed the rat whole. What's on *your* mind?"

"Not eating rats. That's for sure." She looked a little green.

"Are you okay?"

"Fine and dandy. But I have a surprise." She looked around at the family gathered here for the celebration. "I'm glad my grandmother could make it here from L.A. for the wedding."

"Not fair. Don't start something without finishing it. What's the surprise?" He knew they couldn't get away right now for a honeymoon—not with the new foals expected at any moment. So he couldn't imagine what she had planned.

She took both his hands in hers and gazed up into his eyes. Sam had never seen so much love directed at him.

It brought tears to his eyes. "What?"

"I'm trying to decide what you'd want most."

"What are you talking about? Come on, give."

"Another boy or a girl?"

"Horses? They're called colts and fillies. And I think the vet said…"

"No." She poked him in the ribs and laughed. "Not horses. Humans. Baby humans."

For the first time since they'd come back to the ranch, Grace had succeeded in rendering him speechless.

When he finally got his senses back he said, "Seriously? We're... You and me...?"

"Definitely. Are you happy about it?"

"Delirious. I'm, well—stupidly happy about it."

The smile on her face made him desperate to kiss her. So he did. In front of the whole world, he took his bride in his arms and kissed her with the passion of a man who was fantastically, happily and stupidly in love.

His life had turned to gold without him noticing. He was the luckiest S.O.B. in the whole world. All that had once been sad and dreary was now magical and magnificent.

* * * * *

SUSPENSE

Harlequin® ROMANTIC SUSPENSE

COMING NEXT MONTH
AVAILABLE APRIL 24, 2012

#1703 HER HERO AFTER DARK
H.O.T. Watch.
Cindy Dees

#1704 THE PERFECT OUTSIDER
Perfect, Wyoming
Loreth Anne White

#1705 TEXAS MANHUNT
Chance, Texas
Linda Conrad

#1706 IT STARTED THAT NIGHT
Virna DePaul

REQUEST YOUR FREE BOOKS!
2 FREE NOVELS PLUS 2 FREE GIFTS!

ROMANTIC
S U S P E N S E

Sparked by Danger, Fueled by Passion.

YES! Please send me 2 FREE Harlequin® Romantic Suspense novels and my 2 FREE gifts (gifts are worth about $10). After receiving them, if I don't wish to receive any more books, I can return the shipping statement marked "cancel." If I don't cancel, I will receive 4 brand-new novels every month and be billed just $4.49 per book in the U.S. or $5.24 per book in Canada. That's a saving of at least 14% off the cover price! It's quite a bargain! Shipping and handling is just 50¢ per book in the U.S. and 75¢ per book in Canada.* I understand that accepting the 2 free books and gifts places me under no obligation to buy anything. I can always return a shipment and cancel at any time. Even if I never buy another book, the two free books and gifts are mine to keep forever.

240/340 HDN FEFR

Name (PLEASE PRINT)

Address Apt. #

City State/Prov. Zip/Postal Code

Signature (if under 18, a parent or guardian must sign)

Mail to the **Reader Service:**
IN U.S.A.: P.O. Box 1867, Buffalo, NY 14240-1867
IN CANADA: P.O. Box 609, Fort Erie, Ontario L2A 5X3

Not valid for current subscribers to Harlequin Romantic Suspense books.

Want to try two free books from another line?
Call 1-800-873-8635 or visit www.ReaderService.com.

* Terms and prices subject to change without notice. Prices do not include applicable taxes. Sales tax applicable in N.Y. Canadian residents will be charged applicable taxes. Offer not valid in Quebec. This offer is limited to one order per household. All orders subject to credit approval. Credit or debit balances in a customer's account(s) may be offset by any other outstanding balance owed by or to the customer. Please allow 4 to 6 weeks for delivery. Offer available while quantities last.

Your Privacy—The Reader Service is committed to protecting your privacy. Our Privacy Policy is available online at www.ReaderService.com or upon request from the Reader Service.

We make a portion of our mailing list available to reputable third parties that offer products we believe may interest you. If you prefer that we not exchange your name with third parties, or if you wish to clarify or modify your communication preferences, please visit us at www.ReaderService.com/consumerchoice or write to us at Reader Service Preference Service, P.O. Box 9062, Buffalo, NY 14269. Include your complete name and address.

HRS11B

*Colby Investigator Lyle McCaleb is on the case.
But can he protect Sadie Gilmore from her haunting past?*

*Harlequin Intrigue® presents a new installment
in Debra Webb's miniseries,* COLBY, TX.

Enjoy a sneak peek of COLBY LAW.

With the shotgun hanging at her side, she made it as far as the porch steps, when the driver's side door opened. Sadie knew the deputies in Coryell County. Her visitor wasn't any of them. A boot hit the ground, stirring the dust. Something deep inside her braced for a new kind of trouble. As the driver emerged, Sadie's gaze moved upward, over the gleaming black door and the tinted window to a black Stetson and dark sunglasses. She couldn't quite make out the details of the man's face but some extra sense that had nothing to do with what she could see set her on edge.

Another boot hit the ground and the door closed. Her visual inspection swept over long legs cinched in comfortably worn denim, a lean waist and broad shoulders testing the seams of a shirt that hadn't come off the rack at any store where she shopped, finally zeroing in on the man's face just as he removed the dark glasses.

The weapon almost slipped from her grasp. Her heart bucked hard twice, then skidded to a near halt.

Lyle McCaleb.

"What the…devil?" whispered past her lips.

Unable to move a muscle, she watched in morbid fascination as he hooked the sunglasses on to his hip pocket and strode toward the house—toward her. Sadie wouldn't have been able to summon a warning that he was trespassing had her life depended on it.

Lyle glanced at the shotgun as he reached up and removed his hat. "Expecting company?"

As if her heart had suddenly started to pump once more, kicking her brain into gear, fury blasted through her frozen muscles. "What do you want, Lyle McCaleb?"

"Seeing as you didn't know I was coming, that couldn't be for me." He gave a nod toward her shotgun.

This could not be happening. Seven years he'd been gone. This was…this was… "I have nothing to say to you." She turned her back to him and walked away. Who did he think he was, showing up here like this after all this time? It was crazy. He was crazy!

"I know I'm the last person on this earth you want to see."

Her feet stopped when she wanted to keep going. To get inside the house and slam the door and dead bolt it.

"We need to talk."

The stakes are high as Lyle fights for the woman he loves. But can he solve the case in time to save an innocent life?

Find out in COLBY LAW
Available May 2012 from Harlequin Intrigue®
wherever books are sold.

The heartwarming conclusion of

from fan-favorite author
TINA LEONARD

With five brothers married, Jonas Callahan is under no pressure to tie the knot. But when Sabrina McKinley admits her bouncing baby boy is his, Jonas does everything he can to win over the woman he's loved for years. First the last Callahan bachelor must uncover an important family secret…before he can take the lovely Sabrina down the aisle!

A Callahan Wedding

Available this May
wherever books are sold.

www.Harlequin.com

HAR75405

Harlequin *Desire*

ALWAYS POWERFUL, PASSIONATE AND PROVOCATIVE.

ALL IT TAKES IS ONE PASSIONATE NIGHT....

NEW YORK TIMES AND *USA TODAY*
BESTSELLING AUTHOR

MAYA BANKS

CONCLUDES HER IRRESISTIBLE MINISERIES

PREGNANCY & PASSION

Pippa Laingley has one man on her mind: hard-
driving Cameron Hollingsworth. So when Cam
proposes one commitment-free night of passion,
Pippa jumps at the chance. But an unexpected
pregnancy turns no-strings-attached into a tangled
web of emotion. Will Cam feel trapped into reliving
the painful losses of his past or will irrepressible Pippa
break down the walls around his heart and lay claim
to him…once and for all?

UNDONE BY HER
TENDER TOUCH

Find out what the heart wants this May!